Diana: The Ghost Biography

A NOVEL

Emma Tennant and Hilary Bailey

Arcadia Books Ltd
15–16 Nassau Street
London w1w 7ab

www.arcadiabooks.co.uk

First published by Bliss Books, an imprint of Arcadia Books 2009
Copyright © Emma Tennant and Hilary Bailey 2009

Emma Tennant and Hilary Bailey have asserted their moral rights to be identified as the authors of
this work in accordance with the Copyright, Designs and Patents Act, 1988.

A catalogue record for this book is available from the British Library.

isbn 978-1-906413-00-2

Typeset in Garamond by MacGuru Ltd
Printed in Finland by WS Bookwell

Arcadia Books supports English PEN, the fellowship of writers who work together to
promote literature and its understanding. English PEN upholds writers' freedoms in Britain
and around the world, challenging political and cultural limits on free expression. To find
out more, visit www.englishpen.org or contact
English PEN, 6–8 Amwell Street, London ec1r 1uq

Arcadia Books distributors are as follows:

in the UK and elsewhere in Europe:
Turnaround Publishers Services
Unit 3, Olympia Trading Estate
Coburg Road
London n22 6tz

in the US and Canada:
Independent Publishers Group
814 N. Franklin Street
Chicago, IL 60610

in Australia:
Tower Books
PO Box 213
Brookvale, NSW 2100

in New Zealand:
Addenda
PO Box 78224
Grey Lynn
Auckland

in South Africa:
Quartet Sales and Marketing
PO Box 1218
Northcliffe
Johannesburg 2115

Arcadia Books is the *Sunday Times* Small Publisher of the Year

CHAPTER ONE

Janet MacDuff was Head Housekeeper for the Royal Household at their summer castle in Scotland, Balmoral on the River Dee. For close on twenty-five years now, sheets and pillowcases and towels, all with their embroidered monogram of the coat of arms of the House of Windsor (or, in the case of Her Majesty the Queen, the initials ER stitched in loops of white silk thread on linen) had been in the care of Janet. The laundry cupboard and general cleaning in the castle were under her exclusive supervision; and housemaids, picked with care from surrounding villages, were accordingly in awe of the brisk, youthful-looking woman who had weathered the storms of royal divorce and disaster with as much calm and good sense as if they had all added up to no more than a disrupted family picnic. Nothing bothered Janet MacDuff: that was how the Scots described the good sense of a servant the Queen held in particular esteem. And if the Queen's own uncertainty in handling her grandsons' shock and misery at Balmoral on hearing of the death of their mother, the late Princess of Wales, had caused a tremor to run through the monarch's solid edifice, the Head Housekeeper had ensured that everything went on as usual in the running of the castle. Sheets were counted, and those ripped or torn sent away to Mrs Walker in Ballater for mending, as the Queen preferred economy to the purchasing of new linen. Eiderdowns (the duvet did not figure at Balmoral) were cleaned and plumped up for the use of family and royal guests. Janet MacDuff herself took charge of the late Princess's wardrobe, cleaning satin pumps with blue tissue paper and folding gowns worn long ago at the time of her engagement, into

1

zipped bags which were then consigned to the vaults. Nothing escaped Janet MacDuff's attention; and visitors or family members who inadvertently left an object behind at Balmoral, found it posted back to them within a week of departure. It was the duty of the Supervisor of the Royal Household, as she saw it, to obliterate all traces of former occupants of this Victorian Gothic castle in the heart of royal Deeside; and it was the housekeeper's genuine belief that the thorough cleaning and throwing-away process which took place immediately succeeding the tragic accident in which the Princess of Wales lost her life, had been of great assistance to the young Princes. Despite tears from the younger Prince and reproofs from the heir to the throne, Janet had persevered, ridding the bedroom, boudoir and sitting rooms most frequented by their mother, of any reminder of her previous existence. Cassette players, an army of fancy handbags and cosmetics by the casefull, were thrown away. It was better this way, so Mrs MacDuff argued – and Her Majesty did not disagree with the policy. The boys would forget all the sooner if these poignant mementoes were nowhere to be seen.

Today, Janet MacDuff paused in her tour of final inspection of the castle bedrooms and went to the window of the White and Gold Room to look out at the gardens and drive. The room, prepared to receive Prince Harry on his return from Bali, was on the first floor, and while it would have been easier for those in charge of carrying the boy on a stretcher if quarters had been made ready downstairs, security risks made this impossible. It might be weeks before the Prince had the plaster on both arms and legs removed, and everything would have to come up the service staircase in answer to a ring of the bell. Janet MacDuff, as so often before, had considered every contingency, and staff were trained in the lifting and transporting of a severely injured young man. The fact that royal duties had prevented the monarch from being at Balmoral to greet her grandson, combined with the absence until tomorrow of the boy's father, the Prince of Wales, gave Janet MacDuff the temporary role of guardian to the young Prince. There was little sign that this additional responsibility was displeasing to the housekeeper – indeed, her unusually relaxed bearing proclaimed the delight of a devoted servant who has known her charge since birth and is confident of his trust in her.

The ambulance came slowly up the drive at Balmoral and came to a halt on gravel freshly raked and bordered by lawns and flower beds. The driver stepped out as the back door of the vehicle was opened carefully and a young orderly, dark-haired and neat in appearance, came out. A nurse followed him, and together with the driver the two helpers began to pull the stretcher towards them.

Janet MacDuff, directly above this scene at the window of the White and Gold Room, turned to make her own descent to the point of arrival of her future charge. Before she did, she turned again once to look out at the blaze of petunias, the spreading trees magnificent in their late summer foliage, and fine climbing roses and clematis of the castle gardens. Surely, Harry would recuperate here quickly, she thought, smoothing her dress and smiling as the crop of red hair that stuck out above the blanketed figure's head on the stretcher came into view; Harry would be superbly cared for here and all traces of his recent near-fatal accident obliterated, just as the former disasters suffered by this unlucky family had been wiped clean. Soon, neither the victim himself nor the ravening Press would have any other than the most cursory memory of Harry's fall.

It was impossible to remember, later, whether the Head Housekeeper's eye had been caught by the nurse accompanying the patient as she looked up at the window of the White and Gold Room – or if it was Mrs MacDuff who had stared just long enough at the woman now standing on the gravel sweep to occasion a quick return of glance. Whichever it was, as Janet reflected later, the look that flew between them appeared to bring about a sudden decision on the part of the nurse. She walked away from the stretcher, borne by the driver and the neat orderly, and made her way sharply to the side of the castle. Here, a turret obtruded and made it impossible for the housekeeper to see what route she had taken – yet the answer became clear only a few seconds later when steps in the corridor announced that she had chosen the side door and steps to arrive on the first floor. She hesitated before entering the White and Gold Room – and Janet MacDuff, robbed of her long-planned greeting of the invalid by the front entrance at Balmoral, stood amazed a moment at the fact of this plain, soberly dressed woman standing before her as the stretcher was brought up the main stairs and carried in. Then, in the excitement of greeting the battered Prince and ringing for orange squash and peaches from the greenhouses to be placed on a tray for His Royal Highness, Janet MacDuff forgot all about her surprise a short time earlier. Harry had outlined his beloved Scottish castle to the nurse, doubtless, on the long flight home. He'd asked to keep Sister Julia, as she was apparently known, for the duration of his convalescence. Eager to find convenient ways of going in and out without the risk of bumping into a denizen of the castle, the nurse had run round to a side door. There would be plenty of time for the Head Housekeeper to make it quite clear which staircases and rooms at the castle were available for the attendant's use. If Janet MacDuff had taken against the young Prince's carer from the minute of her arrival in the Prince's sickroom, she certainly gave no evidence of it.

CHAPTER TWO

Julia sat on the bed in her small, sparsely furnished room at Balmoral, and for a long time she was silent and motionless, as if the effort of past days had drained her of all her capacity to go on. The long flight home from Bali, after a tense twenty-four hours in the hospital – this, thankfully, more modern in its technology than anything to be found in the camp where she worked in Pakistan, but suffering from a breakdown in electricity caused by a recent typhoon – combined with extreme anxiety at the condition of the young Prince, had taken their toll. Sleep, even in the curtained-off first class section of the 777 accorded to the Queen's grandson, had been impossible; and all through the long dark hours as Asia lay invisible below and a glimmer of a setting sun could be seen over the deserts of the Middle East, Julia had remained, silent and alert as she was now, by the side of her sedated patient. From time to time she permitted herself a long, troubled glance at the young man she couldn't help thinking of as a boy, spiky red hair as untamed as it had been when he was still under thirteen years old and skin fresh and smooth as when he had been a baby, but the slightest movement in the cabin caused a shrinking back into the shadows, and a stewardess passing with trays of orange juice found herself dismissed with a faint shake of the head from the Prince's attendant. After the eminent neurosurgeon Dr Van Hage disembarked at Karachi to resume the tour, interrupted by Harry's fall, of hospitals and medical aid centres in Pakistan and India, the calm and silence enveloping Sister Julia grew deeper still, and she and the Prince were left undisturbed until Europe gleamed green thirty-five thousand feet

5

down. For those hours, together and alone in the grey half-light of the cabin, Sister Julia and Harry breathed in the same light rhythm and their eyes flickered open and closed at intervals, as if prompted by the same strange dream.

Arrival at Heathrow belonged also in the blur of the last few days. News had leaked of the Prince's flight from Bali after the bungee-jumping accident and his imminent arrival following what was already described as a life-saving operation, and the stretchered figure had to be hustled, along with the plain brown-haired woman taken to be his nurse, from aircraft steps to a waiting ambulance. A blinding sheet of light from photographers' flashes went off as the doors of the ambulance closed; and Julia, crouched now still on the edge of the narrow bed in her sparsely furnished room at Balmoral, shuddered as the scene came back to her. It had been close to being another chase, this time with a wounded royal pursued all the way north by a posse of motorbike-riding paparazzi – and she knew now that this had been the hardest part of the traumatic days she had just lived through. Her instinct had been to throw herself from the ambulance and vanish forever. But another instinct proved stronger, in the end; and she had stayed with the Prince, leaning over and wiping his pale sweat-bathed cheeks as they pounded down the motorway. She heard the racing engines of the Press bikes and cars; then there was silence. Orders must have been given to let the Prince alone on his journey to convalesce at the castle, and because this was England, they had been obeyed. But Julia flinched as she thought of the journey, and it was with effort that she reminded herself of the joy she had felt when her patient opened his eyes for the first time, little more than an hour ago. He had been happy – so it was clear to those in the sickroom – when he observed his surroundings; and, as Tibbie the Scottish head housemaid working under Mrs Janet MacDuff had remarked, he had directed a very sweet smile in the direction of the nurse who stood patiently away from the rest of the welcoming committee. 'He's lucky to have her,' Tibbie announced in Julia's hearing as the housekeeper and maid left the room. Janet MacDuff gave no reply that Julia could hear, and for the first time in all the thousands of miles she had travelled and all the anguish and fear she had felt, the woman known as Sister Julia broke down in tears at the memory of MacDuff's cold glance at their first encounter, and her peremptory dismissal. She had known it a mistake, to run up the side stairs at the castle and obtain entry, that way – but surely it was not such a crime? The hostility of Janet MacDuff had affected Julia more than anything, in all she had suffered on this visit to a country she had never thought to see again. It was as if a long-forgotten wound, one far worse than any physical injuries she had endured in her past life, had been opened up, and there might never be a way of healing it again.

Julia wept; and as she did so she felt the relief of letting go. *Past, present and future were joined in a blur. Where would she go after this? The refugee camp where she had lived and worked seemed miles away and life here impossible.* She would dedicate her life to others – as she always had. But for the first time in her life, Julia saw no way forward without a return of at least some of the love she so freely gave. Her thoughts, held back over the years, went irresistibly to two boys, men now of course, but boys for her still in her heart. And she wept again, allowing the tears to pour down her face unchecked.

Footsteps on the hard cord allotted to quarters in the staff wing of the castle, sounded loud and impatient in the corridor. There was a tap at the door, and Julia had only a second in which to dive to the bag on the floor and pull out a tissue.

Tibbie stood in the doorway, unsmiling. 'Her Majesty the Queen comes up on the royal train tonight,' Tibbie announced. 'Mrs MacDuff requires you to have His Royal Highness Prince Harry ready and bathed by seven a.m. tomorrow and the bed linen changed by six thirty.'

Julia rose, as if the Queen herself had uttered this command. Then, as Tibbie closed the door and her footsteps receded down the long passage, she went over to the window and looked out at the formal gardens of the castle and the neatly raked gravel paths.

CHAPTER THREE

Balmoral readied itself for the Queen's arrival long before daybreak. Nights were brief at this time of year in Scotland, and the blue light of what could be taken for an unending gloaming, filled the rooms and lofty halls with the promise of dawn long before it was time. A three-quarter moon stared unabashedly into Julia's modest sliver of bed, wooden chair and cupboard, and it illuminated also the royal suite on the first floor of the castle which the monarch and her consort would occupy. Prince Harry, in his room fitted with hospital equipment, was at the back and slept soundly.

Julia was the first to hear the preparations for an early breakfast, and to shrink back, also, for a moment under the covers at the unmistakable sound of Mrs MacDuff's footsteps in the passage outside. It was too soon to wake her patient – like any adolescent (although she knew him to be more than that) – the boy slept in at the best of times. And it was too late (she should have crept to the sickroom when it was still properly night) to risk another encounter with the housekeeper by venturing outside her room. There was no choice, Julia ruefully accepted, but to lie on in the narrow bed supplied, by the feel and look of it, to the Royal Household at the time of Queen Victoria, and pretend to herself that she was at rest.

Thoughts came, however, and they were hard to resist. They led Julia first to the study where the Queen wrote and answered letters. Hadn't Mary the maid led her in there yesterday and pointed to the pile of correspondence, set to one side, which expressed condolence and concern over Prince Harry's recent bungee-jumping accident – and hadn't Mary burst out laughing when the nurse clapped her hand over her mouth as if she'd seen a ghost there? 'Mrs MacDuff says you're to take the cards and stuff along to HRH when Her Majesty's read them,' the maid went on, her voice fading away at the realisation that Julia had left the study abruptly. 'You're no to forget!' she called down the corridor after her.

Now Julia imagined the small room with its elegant lacquered escritoire, each pigeon-hole neatly labelled – and its thick plush curtains, another relic of Victoria's days, which made a setting both theatrical and forbidding for its royal occupant. She shrank even further at the vision, unbidden and unwelcome, of the Queen settled at her desk, her secretary standing to one side, pad and slimline pen poised for dictation. The carefully coiffeured white curls swung round – and Julia woke, aware as she forced herself upright that reality and dream had become indistinguishable: the letters from an anxious, loving public were physically in the Queen's boudoir – as Julia had been the day before, with wee Mary – but Her Majesty certainly was not yet in residence. The royal train would barely have crossed the border by now – but the thoughts which came after this were unbearable to Julia and she found herself dressing with as much urgency as if the fire brigade had been summoned to the castle and she had no more than a few seconds to go before immolation or death. The train, with the early light coming in through the windows and the long, quiet stops engineered in order to increase the comfort of the reigning sovereign as she rested or slept, continued to haunt Julia until she was out in the corridor and making her way to the rear of the building. MacDuff or not, she would go, as silently as possible, to Harry's sickroom. His was the only presence which proved a solace, stranger as she was in this mausoleum to the past glories of the realm.

All was quiet on the journey along the tributaries – passages as dark as rivers and hung with portraits of long-dead statesmen and their wives – and there was silence, too, in the wide open spaces, dizzying in their vastness as deserts, of the great stronghold that is Balmoral. Julia neither saw nor heard Mrs MacDuff: neither Mary, nor John the Head Footman, bringer of Harry's daily meals on a tray from the cavernous kitchens below, were in evidence. It was almost, you might say, as if this northernmost palace of a still-powerful dynasty had been abandoned, and could do little but await its end.

That the action took place elsewhere in the castle occurred to Julia, and she paused before walking the last stretch, across a long, wide landing. Here were rooms apportioned to the most distinguished guests, each looking out on heathered slopes, a rushing burn and pine forests which climbed to the horizon. The White and Gold Room where Harry was quartered, was one of these; and as the growing sounds of the household bustling into a new day prepared to receive the Queen, now reached Julia's ears, she also heard the young Prince's laugh echoing across the landing. She frowned; for it was improbable that a visit from Mrs MacDuff or quiet, dour John, could bring this degree of hilarity. Had some mate from across the world texted Harry with a joke or a cheering message? Julia hoped so.

The door to the White and Gold Room had on its card with golden metal surround the words *HRH Prince Henry of Wales*.

Next door, Julia noted, had substituted a blank square of white cardboard – in place only yesterday – for the name of a new invitee to the castle. It was impossible to resist pausing a moment, to scrutinise the card – and as Julia peered at it, the door of Harry's sickroom swung open.

Mrs Camilla Parker Bowles announced the card, in a strong black ink. Julia turned away from it, a blush rising into her neck and face, and as she did so a figure emerged from the doorway of the White and Gold Room.

'Have you lost your way?' came the quiet, amused tone of the Prince of Wales. 'That can't be the case, surely, if you're who I think you are – Sister Julia, isn't it, who Harry has told me so much about…'

The morning was already half gone by the time Julia had done her morning chores around the young patient. The room was dusted – even wee Mary was not permitted anywhere near the royal convalescent at important times, such as this one, an impending visit from his grandmother, the Queen. Bandages were changed on one hand and both lower arms, and jugs of fresh spring water from Strathmore replenished around the room. The Prince, despite the discomfort of plaster casts on his legs (these already emblazoned with graffiti from other youthful sufferers back in the Bali hospital) appeared, Julia was delighted to observe, more fresh-faced and ruddy with every moment that passed. Her fears for him, still acute, subsided a degree each time she allowed herself a glance at the pink-cheeked, tousle-haired redhead, his face as familiar to millions of Britons as it was to her. 'You're doing fine, Harry,' the quiet nurse murmured from time to time as she adjusted the chart at the end of the bed with its record of his night-time fluctuations in temperature, this ready for Dr McLaren's morning visit. And Harry, comfortable as only Julia could make him, smiled contentedly back from amongst his pillows.

The activity demanded by the coming arrival of the woman Harry revered but also feared – ball games in the long gallery had been sternly discouraged in his childhood, and long hours standing, kilted and obedient, had been required of the boy when he wished only to go fishing for trout in the burn with Colin, a shepherd's son – helped take Julia's attention away from the other occupant of the sickroom, Charles. How she could have borne the presence of a man both distant and apparently over-concerned with every word or gesture made by another – 'Oh yes, how very interesting' would appear to be pro-pelled at some pre-ordained speed from the mouth of the Prince of Wales, Duke of Cornwall, as if the kingdom required the engine of his concern – 'Oh the truth dawns on me that you may be right' – how she could have stayed even a minute in his presence, without the dis-traction of bustle and menial work, Julia could not say. The earnest, downward look of this man so invested with dignity that he had soared, or so she thought, beyond royal status to some other-worldly sphere, led her to keep her eyes down herself, sometimes in sympathy and often enough in pure embarrassment. Harry, who dozed now after his morning medicine, smiled when woken in his father's direction. But altogether there was a soporific atmosphere in the splendid room, the Chippendale gilt chairs and white satin sofas giving off an aura of femininity and luxury that was sadly lacking in the poor lad's life. He needed – there was little doubt about it – a mother at such times. And it was at Julia that the most radiant smiles were directed, despite his father's quiet vigil at his bedside.

The Queen came in, her lady-in-waiting behind her, and the room, gleaming with the good cleaning it had received that morning, seemed to flex its muscles and stand to attention. The Prince of Wales rose – though his arrival in the early hours – and perhaps something else – a painful episode, an altercation of some kind? – lent him a look of weariness. Prince Harry's legs twitched in reflex, under the fine blue eiderdown. Mrs MacDuff, sidling in with John the footman, appeared in the door of the sickroom and they curtsied and bowed.

Julia couldn't have said later why all eyes turned on her at that moment. She was only the nurse, after all – not even a local character known to the Royal Family or kept feudally on the estate in one of the little grey stone houses which pass for cottages in Scotland. She was a stranger, taken up by an orthopaedic surgeon visiting the refugee camp in Pakistan who had noted her skills as a nurse; and she had been transported to this fortress of cold privilege at the insistence of a young Prince accustomed to have his way. Why did the Queen, then, look long and hard at this woman as she performed a deep obeisance? And the housekeeper – why did she too look on as if in astonishment at the expected reverence to a Queen? Only Lady Bannerman, the newly-recruited lady-in-waiting, seemed to see nothing unusual in the way the nurse sank almost to the ground, as if practised over many years in the art of the perfect curtsey. But then Lady Bannerman had no way of knowing when and how the new nurse had come to Balmoral. The greetings didn't have time to begin before a rush of small dogs ran into the room – and it occurred to Julia that it was for precisely this that the Queen's flock of corgis were put to use – the roughing up of too-formal moments, or to gloss over impossible feuds between those close to the throne. The dogs barked; the Queen was able to call reprovingly at them as they attempted to obtrude her passage to the sick-bed; and the showing of love or anxiety for the still-wounded boy was lost in the din.

But there was little time for such imaginings. Her Majesty, ramrod-straight and attired in pale blue cashmere and Stuart hunting tartan skirt, and seemingly as fresh after her journey north by train as her eldest son was exhausted by his night drive, turned to Julia by the side of her grandson's bed. She spoke in the high, clear voice all denizens of her kingdom would recognise, whether willingly or not, as the voice which defined their status as subjects, not citizens: like ice balls thrown together, Julia thought with a shudder, as she steadied herself for a royal interrogation. For this woman many in this country would – still – give their lives. And in her name many do, in wars and quelling riots around the world, on land and sea and air. It was symptomatic of the awe in which this small figure was held that no questioning of Her Majesty's role in assenting to the deployment of forces overseas had yet taken place in Britain, Julia half-thought, staring out across the bed at the high windows, with their view of lush August gardens and innumerable acres of mountainside stretching out under a clear sky. The Queen, for all that the power once invested in the monarchy had been long removed, was a strangely potent emblem – but of what? Julia wondered, as the small face turned from Harry after a stoop to kiss the lad's cheek, to his nurse – what was Her Majesty an emblem of? The past, surely: the future for the Crown was hard to see – unless –

'So, Sister…' The Queen broke into Julia's thoughts; it was unlike her to forget a name, Julia knew that. What had Mrs MacDuff told her of the nurse's past? – did she, even, believe Sister Julia was here on some kind of false pretence? Julia's cheeks flamed at the possibility.

'Sister Julia, ma'am,' she replied in a low voice.

The Queen raised an eyebrow by a fraction. Clearly she had not been supplied with a second name. Mrs MacDuff bustled forward: the awkwardness must be resolved and HM able to continue with her morning in the study answering letters.

'Sister Julia has – she is attached to a charity in Pakistan, Your Majesty,' Mrs MacDuff said.

'Ah,' said the Queen, and one of the smiles for which she was famed, illuminated her features. 'A most worthwhile career. So in your opinion, Sister Julia, His Royal Highness makes good progress here?'

It would have been impossible to say later whether the intervention of the Prince of Wales or the sudden, bounding entrance of another small dog to join those now coiled on the floor, came first: what could be stated with certainty was that the effect of the dog, and Julia and Charles combined, caused immediate chaos in the royal sickroom. 'Whisky!' Charles shouted, as the corgi hurtled through the door and made straight, or so it appeared, for the invalid in the high bed. 'Whisky, down! I do apologise, Sister er…'

The corgi ran to Julia, ears back and tail wagging. Rolling on its back, it stared with undisguised love and yearning, up at the nurse

– and she, imprisoned as she was on one side by the rails of the bed and on the other by the proximity of the boy's father, had no way of escape. 'It appears that Whisky has taken a fancy to Sister Julia,' came the dry-ice tones of the Queen. 'The dogs came up with me on the train, so they cannot have known each other before. How delight-ful,' came the additional comment; and for the first time the monarch appeared to relax in the presence of her son and grandson. The dogs were essential aids to communication, Julia recognised: they must be the sole conduit of true feeling permitted to the monarch and her young. 'Charles, do pull him off,' the Queen said.

Prince Charles's hands, restraining Whisky as he stepped forward and the dog renewed its friendly assault on Julia, grabbed and pulled, to no avail; muttered apologies turned to curses and then finally, once the Prince held the obstreperous beast by the scruff of the neck, to laughter. His eyes met Julia's. Both, for a long moment, stared at each other. 'Bad boy, Whisky,' the Prince said.

The door of the White and Gold Room opened. A face, lit by the several strands of real pearls clasped below and framed by feathery light blonde hair, looked round as if searching for a lost companion. Julia observed the well-known droop of the chin and the humorous, indulgent mouth – and then forced herself to look at the eyes, which now met the Prince's with a reassuring glance. The eyes knew, however, to move on to the Queen, who stood silent and unsmiling on the far side of the bed from Julia. A curtsey took the newcomer's gaze down to floor level, where Whisky stayed immobile, with neither recognition nor interest at the entrance of Camilla Parker Bowles.

CHAPTER FOUR

David Baron's room at Balmoral was not charming. Square, not very large and overlooking the kitchen gardens, it contained a bed with an art deco carved headboard, showing some dreamlike draped figures, an Edwardian walnut tallboy and a Victorian buttoned chair, all shouting, 'too good to throw away'. The dark green fitted carpet, though, was new and the small bathroom well appointed. Baron had, the night before, put his things, including a large bottle of very expensive aftershave, said to be used by David Beckham, in there. He had also unpacked one suitcase. Now he was unpacking the second, which stood open on a table by the window.

He crossed the room smoothly, carrying a dinner jacket in a plastic cleaner's bag. He put it neatly into a fitted wardrobe. Baron was a tall, slender man with broad shoulders. He moved easily and was economical in his movements. As a boy he had won medals for swimming. He checked the pager in his pocket, then walked to the walnut mirror over the fireplace. He studied his appearance with some attention. His oval face was close-shaven, his dark brown hair was neatly trimmed, the whites of his long hazel eyes were clear. He had a supple, narrow-lipped mouth. He straightened his tie, went back to his suitcase and carefully took out a pair of khaki GAP trousers.

He checked the pager again. He was half-expecting a call. He had arrived at Balmoral in the late afternoon and arranged the Prince's suite. The Prince and Mrs Parker Bowles had arrived in the middle of the night. Now, soon after breakfast, was the moment when any errors in his arrangements would be mentioned. The temperature in a room

17

might be unsatisfactory. Something – a photograph, an ornament, a gift – which ought to have been brought from Clarence House might not be there. Alternatively, there might be something unwanted in one of the rooms, a picture, for example. Agreed, the Prince had occupied the same rooms at Balmoral on countless occasions but it was some time since he had resided there. Birkhill, the house on the estate left to him by his grandmother, was at present uninhabitable as major restorations were taking place. There was still the chance of a mistake. The day before Baron had personally overseen the two footmen effortfully carrying upstairs a full length portrait, swathed in an old velvet curtain, showing Camilla Parker Bowles's great grandmother, Alice Keppel, in court dress – satin, a fan, pearls. He had seen this put in place on a wall in the Prince's drawing room but there was every chance it might have to be moved.

The phone rang in the pocket of Baron's jacket, which hung on the back of the chair by the desk. Only four people had Baron's mobile phone number.

'How are you, dear heart?' said a light, amused voice. Baron pictured the speaker, sitting at the long bench of workstations, jacket off, sleeves rolled up, bright blue eyes probably screwed up after a long night. In front of him there would be a heap of invitation cards and another pile of press releases.

'Sebastian,' Baron said urgently, 'listen, Sebastian, I thought we'd agreed it wouldn't be a good idea to ring me here.' He had the unpleasant sensation of sweat on his brow and pricking in his hair. He was panicking. The trouble with Sebastian, he thought, was that he'd more or less modelled himself on another Sebastian, the louche, aristocratic hero of *Brideshead Revisited*. He had the looks, Baron thought, even if he didn't have the broad acres, the private chapel or the religion. He lacked the fictional Sebastian's vices, also. This Sebastian drank little and didn't use drugs. His pretended idleness masked energy and ambition. But Baron feared that Sebastian had now dropped into one of his mock-aristocratic insouciant poses, which Baron dreaded.

'Sebastian,' he appealed again. He was Prince Charles's most favoured equerry. Sebastian was a gossip columnist of a daily tabloid newspaper. It was not his fault, thought Baron. He had met Sebastian at a party – they had fallen in love as soon as they saw each other but, because each for his own reasons wanted to conceal what he did for a living, they had both lied about their jobs. By the time they told each other the truth it was too late. So he, Baron, was in a close relationship with a tabloid journalist. To any member of the Royal Family this would seem an unholy alliance, on a par, among ordinary people, with finding your wife in bed with your brother. 'It's out of order, Seb,' he said. '"Private's private," we said'. He dared not be more explicit. Who knew who was listening?

'I only wanted a gossip,' said Baron's blond lover in a conciliatory tone. 'There's nothing doing here – I'm idle.'

Baron jumped on him, 'I'll be idle, too, if you aren't careful,' he said rapidly. 'As in unemployed. Got it?'

'Got it,' Sebastian said without emphasis. 'Love you.'

'Love you, too,' Baron said in a quick mutter. In his mind's eye he saw the conversation being played over in a room full of grinning MI6 officers. He was relieved when Sebastian broke the connection. He exhaled, checked his pager yet again and then rapidly put away the rest of his clothes. All that was left on the table was an attractively wrapped box. This he picked up and left the room.

Downstairs in the servants' part of the castle he knocked on a solid, varnished door with a brass doorknob. A voice inside responded and Baron entered Janet MacDuff's sanctum. The housekeeper was sitting at a desk at the back of her cosy sitting room. Although there was a computer on the desk beside her, she was working on a large ledger with a big fountain pen. On one small Edwardian table stood silver framed photographs of Mrs MacDuff with the Queen and of two laughing, kilted boys on a moor – the Princes William and Harry. On another table stood more photographs – one of a younger Mrs MacDuff with a heavy-set kilted man, perhaps her father, perhaps the late Mr MacDuff, another of two tough-looking crop headed young men in regimental uniforms, the MacDuff sons.

Mrs MacDuff smiled when Baron came in. She stood up. 'Welcome back, Mr Baron. Welcome back indeed.'

'It's always a pleasure to be here,' he replied. He put the wrapped box into her hands. 'No surprises,' he said, 'but I was going past Fortnums and I thought of you and your *marrons glacés*.'

'It's a terrible weakness,' said Mrs MacDuff. 'And it's wicked of you to indulge me.'

'You're entitled to a little treat from time to time,' Baron told her. 'Would you like some tea, or perhaps a cup of coffee?' she asked. 'No time, Janet,' he answered. 'You know what it's like – who better?'

'Well, come and sit down, Mr Baron,' she said. They sat down comfortably on either side of the fireplace and settled for a confidential chat, the hardworking, trusted housekeeper and the soothing, attentive young equerry.

Baron leaned forward. 'Now – how have you been keeping, Janet?' he asked.

'Very well,' she responded. 'But it's been an awful business, this accident of Prince Harry's. My knees turned to water when I heard. To think – he might have been killed! What were they thinking of?'

'There's been a good deal of extra work for you, I suppose?'

'We coped,' she said.

'I'm sure you did,' he assured her. 'You always do.' Baron allowed a silence to fall. Mrs MacDuff had something to impart. He knew it.

'There's a nurse – ' she said.

'A nurse?' Baron echoed.

'She came with Prince Harry. He's very attached to her, so they say.'

It was plain to Baron that Mrs MacDuff disliked the nurse, which did not much surprise him. She was always hostile to staff she thought were gaining too much influence with the Royal Family. When possible, she got rid of them. Prince Harry's nurse, though, would be outside her area of control.

'There's something you don't like about her?' he asked.

'There's something wrong,' said Janet MacDuff. 'The first thing she did, when Prince Harry's ambulance arrived, was get out and disappear to the rear of the castle. Next thing, Mary said, she was in the sickroom checking everything. She must have taken the stairs at the back – but how did she know? Now, she's walking about as if she owned the place. She's a mousey wee thing with nothing to say for herself, but she knows the castle, I'm sure of it. And do you know what she did this morning? Rang up to speak to me and asks, "Mrs MacDuff – I wonder if you could ask Jimmy to produce some asparagus for Prince Harry's lunch." Giving me my orders, you see, and how would she know it was Mr Reid I'd have to ask – and calling him

"Jimmy" like that. Impertinent, you see, in spite of all that eyes-to-the-ground meekness. I don't like it. There's something not right about her. Mary, mind you, is practically in love with her, the silly wee thing. She says she's never seen such devotion. Devotion!' Mrs MacDuff said scornfully, 'What need has he of devotion? He has the best surgeons, the best doctors and a London physiotherapist coming in daily. Not to mention Her Majesty, the Prince of Wales himself and, of course, Mrs Parker Bowles – why would he require all this devotion from a stranger, a woman from nowhere?'

She paused, thinking perhaps she had gone too far. Then she said, in a lower tone, 'Even Whisky was all over her this morning, in Prince Harry's sickroom. He got himself into quite a state.'

Baron sat silently, head on one side, waiting.

Mrs MacDuff shook her head. 'There's something I can't put my finger on,' she said. Baron considered what she had said and took it fairly seriously. He knew from experience that, even if she had prejudices against certain kinds of staff, she also appeared to be psychically tuned into the castle, into its fabric, into everything it contained and into every person within the walls. The cosy, old-fashioned sitting room was filled with Mrs MacDuff's secrets and intuitions.

'I trust your instincts – ' he said, but at that moment his pager went off. He pulled it from his pocket. 'No rest for the wicked,' he remarked and went to the phone on Mrs MacDuff's desk. 'May I?' he asked, and dialled an internal number. 'Baron, Your Royal Highness,' he said, then listened. 'Yes, of course, sir,' he said. He listened again and replied, 'It can be done by the early afternoon.' The voice at the other end said something else. 'Yes, sir, by after lunch.' He put the phone down and looked at it for a second or two. Then he turned to Janet MacDuff. 'I shall need your help, Janet,' he said. 'His Royal Highness wants all his and Mrs Parker Bowles's things moved to the Lodge. Asap. Can you talk to Mr Simpson for me? I'll need some footmen. Two maids – and Hamish.'

'The Prince saw his father today in the North drawing room after breakfast,' she told him without expression.

'Oh,' Baron said. The time of the summons, and the place, meant that Prince Philip might have decided to tell his son, forcibly, something his son did not want to hear. This, even in the best of families, can lead to disagreements and it looked to Baron and Mrs MacDuff, as if in this case it had.

After Baron had left Mrs MacDuff went to her desk and used the telephone to organise staff to assist with the removal. When she'd finished she sat down again at her desk and picked up her pen. For a moment she stared ahead of her, frowning. What had Prince Philip said to the Prince of Wales, or the Prince of Wales to his father, to cause the sudden move to the shooting lodge some two miles from the castle? She couldn't work it out, and turned back to her ledger.

Baron, in the drawing room of the Prince's suite was, as he looked about him to plan the removal, wondering just the same thing. Unlike Janet MacDuff, he had an idea, the beginnings of a theory. 'It's something to do with the marriage,' he said to himself.

Baron knew what quite a lot of people knew, although the great British public, so far, did not and, if it had, would probably have had difficulty in understanding what it all meant. Baron, though, did know and, as the son of a Church of England clergyman, had no difficulty in construing the matter. For three months now the Archbishop of Canterbury had been discreetly canvassing the opinions of his bishops, from York to Hong Kong, to see if they would support the proposal that in future the Church of England would marry, in church, people who had been divorced. The fact that the Church would not do this had helped precipitate the Abdication crisis in the 1930s. The Prince of Wales, destined to be Head of the Church of England when he became King, would be able, in the Church he was about to lead, to marry Mrs Parker Bowles, a divorcee. If the Church of England did not alter its rules, he could never marry her. It would be unthinkable to have the future Head of the Church of England married by the Church of Scotland, or, for that matter, by the state, in a register office. Unthinkable, illegal, unconstitutional – completely out of the question. 'Something to do with the marriage,' Baron pondered. 'But what?' He didn't know.

Sir James Potter, the Prince's Private Secretary, looked in. 'Everything under control, Baron?' he asked.

'Cars, helpers and the invaluable Hamish are all on their way,' Baron assured him.

'Good man,' said Sir James, and left the room. He seemed as imperturbable as ever, but Baron had noted lines of strain around his mouth. Minutes later two footmen entered, carrying between them a large wooden crate. Two others followed, similarly burdened. Then two maids. Baron began to give his orders. Finally, in came Hamish Sutherland, an elderly man in a brown apron. Baron gestured to the picture of Mrs Keppel, calm and slightly smiling above the lace cascading from her bosom.

'Will you take the portrait down, Hamish?' he said. 'And then see it wrapped. It has to go up in the drawing room at the Lodge.'

'Certainly, Mr Baron,' Hamish replied impassively.

David Baron stood in the drawing room at the Lodge. Four crates lay half-empty on the carpet. One maid was carrying plates, one by one, to the kitchen. Another was making up the bed in the Prince's room. Hamish was standing at the top of a ladder propped against the wall opposite the windows, which looked, across a road, at a great sweep of empty moorland. Two footmen unswathed the portrait and heaved it up towards Hamish, steadying it as he attached it to the hooks on the wall. Hamish gave the top of the picture a little tug, to test its firmness, then began to come down the ladder. Baron bent over and pulled a small package, in tissue paper, from one of the crates. He unwrapped it. Two jewel-encrusted Fabergé eggs glittered up at him. He put them gently on a table.

'Thank you, Hamish,' he said. 'You might as well go and wait in the car for the others. Lunch will be at the castle.' He rapidly ordered the disposition of the items without which the Prince never travelled – the silver cutlery, the photographs, the tapestried footstool covered by Queen Mary, a small escritoire which had belonged to his grandmother. He accepted the flowers which had been delivered and gave them to a maid to put in water. He checked the bathrooms to make quite sure each had the correct soap and lotions in it. It was done surprisingly quickly, with many practised hands at work. Soon the men were carrying out the emptied crates and the maid who was to remain at the Lodge began to vacuum the floor. Baron thanked the others and sent them off to get their midday meal at the castle. Later, some would return, with a chef and provisions.

Baron stayed behind, brooding. The sky had begun to cloud over, dark shadows were sweeping down over the moor. 'The wedding

– Charles wants to set a date and his father won't allow it,' he decided, the sound of the vacuum cleaner in his ears.

He went outside and climbed into the jeep. He would drive down the glen to the castle and the road needed a four-wheel drive. Would the estate agree finally to pay for it? Baron wondered – he might bring up the subject with the Prince of Wales later. For now, Charles was out sketching up at Loch Shiel and Camilla had gone for a walk.

Baron let out the clutch and the jeep rolled down over heather and moss to the glen road.

CHAPTER FIVE

Julia couldn't have said, later, how the small crowd of concerned relatives circling her young charge's bed had dispersed. The Queen had, of course, been first to leave, with her lady-in-waiting in tow and Mrs MacDuff and John flattened against the wall as she went by like – so Julia remembered thinking – visitors caught in a funfair Wall of Death. There had been a bustling – as McKendrick, the under-butler, swept in to announce the arrival of the local doctor and wee Mary, dropping on hands and knees to remove Kleenex balls tossed down by the patient onto the floor, ducked and dived to avoid collision. The dogs, yapping with pleasure at a promised walk, rushed out after their royal owner. Then Dr McLaren was finally there, and looking gravely at the temperature chart as he enquired of 'Sister Julia' whether or not the Prince – who dozed now again, tired from all the commotion – had experienced pain during the night. How Prince Charles and the woman the more disapproving Scottish church members termed his mistress, had disappeared from the scene, it was hard to say. Julia knew only that she glanced over at the place near the door where they had been standing together since the entrance of Camilla – this after answering the doctor as best she could on the subject of the improving condition of Prince Harry – and the pair had gone. They hadn't glanced at her, certainly – but then royals didn't look directly at servants; and the unknown Julia from a charity aid base in Pakistan was little more than a servant. Indeed, she was probably rather less. There had been one occasion in the tussle with the dog, when the father of the injured boy had looked straight into her eyes, it was true. But,

25

while Julia thought repeatedly of that gaze, turning it over in her mind as if examination would produce evidence of recognition for the services she performed for his son – or an unease caused by the sense that they had, just possibly, met or known each other in some way – she felt sure that neither reaction was remotely probable. The Prince had, quite simply, already forgotten their brief encounter.

These thoughts possessed Julia as she walked. She was out, away from the pomp and stifling vastness of Balmoral; and with each step she took she removed herself, in turn, from the complications and hidden motives of this difficult family. She went – rather, her feet took her along as if in response to some long-forgotten command – on the road, more of a track really, stony and unmade, leading up a glen on the east of the estate. A fine valley, thick with larch trees on the higher slopes of the hills, and silver birch in abundance. As she walked, flocks of young partridges ran across the track, and she held back for them to pass before walking by the beds of bracken where they'd risen, disturbed by the unusual sound of tramping feet. Julia, looking down at the brown and grey chicks, long-legged, beautiful, suffered a pang as they rushed down the road before her. No one – nothing – knew her, here: she left as little mark on the place as these half-wild birds did. The guns would be out for them in October, she thought, and she pushed the self-pitying question which followed, to one side: what would have become of *her*, by then, if the doctor's prognosis was correct and Harry was off his crutches before summer was gone? How could she leave him and Balmoral – and how could she stay?

Julia paused about a mile on, when a small grey stone house came into view. Separated from the rough land she walked through by a small burn and an arched bridge, the house, a shepherd's cottage, had neat grass lawns in front and a walled area to the side where flowers and fruit trees made an orderly array. This, Julia thought as she stood by the bridge, gazing down at the clear water running over brown pebbles – this is where we could have been happy. Perhaps. A simple sitting room downstairs, a box bed upstairs where we could draw the curtains across and listen to the rain come down. No formal dinners, no fawning courtiers, no smiling rival dictating the order of events.

But she knew this for the fantasy it was. Those born to be royal had no choice but to remain royal all their lives. What would be said of the heir to the still-revered throne if he elected to live like a shepherd, relishing solitude, out in all weather, putting his feet up by a peat or moss fire in the evening, with a book? It was impossible to contemplate.

As Julia stood dreaming, her attention drawn by the rich, heraldic colours of the wild nasturtiums growing on the banks of the fast-flowing water, she became aware of a figure making its way across the neat cottage lawn towards the bridge. She straightened from picking an orange and a yellow flower for Harry's sickroom and binding them together with a dock leaf to make a posy. The sun came out from behind a cloud and dazzled her eyes, so the figure seemed tall one moment, strange and lopsided the next – and with her hand she shaded her gaze until it came closer. A sheepdog – a black and white border collie – ran ahead of the approaching man – for this, at least, Julia could see he was. Then, stopping in its tracks, it stood and sniffed the air. The man stopped too; and then, seeing Julia, he ran towards her with arms outstretched. The collie slunk off, as if ashamed of its companion's sudden, wild gesture.

Julia felt not fear, but a sinking of the heart that was more painful than fear itself. It was the apprehension of what came running to her that churned her stomach and caused her whole body to tremble, as if threatened by mortal danger. She had neither the will nor the ability to flee. 'So –' she murmured as her pulse calmed a little and her brain raced – 'he came to this!'

There was no time for any further thought or comment, now. The figure that had just emerged from the neat cottage was about nineteen years old. He was as unkempt and unshaven as the shepherd's homestead was ordered and clean, and he was, as Julia noted with another surge of dread at the wreck of a fine young man who stood before her, almost mad-looking, with his glazed, bloodshot eyes that were incapable of focusing. A strange sideways loping walk that had given the impression, at a distance, of a twisted body or broken bones, appeared to be the result of an incessant desire to move – in any direction, even while walking – and this consisted of jumping to right and left or up and down like a jack-in-the-box. Julia's heart bled for the boy – and, her strength and resolve restored, she ran across the arched bridge to meet him.

It was long – so long since anyone had taken the efficient, unproud nurse in their arms, that Julia felt the tears, stronger than those she had shed last night on her bed in the castle, but sweeter and at last happy, as they ran down her cheeks and landed on Colin the shepherd's son's filthy and tattered Arran knit. He cried, too: and with slurred speech he pronounced his delight at her coming to him. She was a dream, an apparition to him, Julia knew, and she wondered at the cruelty of those who had failed to respond to Colin's obvious and desperate needs. The poor boy! – he was in need of instant care and treatment... Julia must arrange it, all her old instincts told her, and without delay.

The quiet, brown-haired woman who walked into the shepherd's house with her arms round a stumbling, raving addict, was seen from a four-wheel drive jeep as it made its way up the valley towards the royal Lodge. The driver of the jeep, a dark-haired man in an expensive suit of Scottish tweed, slowed and stared out across the burn and the mown grass at the couple as they went in under the porch and disappeared from sight.

Inside the small stone house all was methodically arranged – with the exception of a room at the back, more of a larder leading off a simple kitchen, which was clearly Colin's home. Julia wondered if he had been relegated there by a father at his wits' end: what had Colin done, to deserve such punishment?

The answer appeared to lie in the jumble of objects strewn around the dark, stone-floored annex: broken record players, a tangle of Sony Walkman and computer parts; a couple of mini TV sets, one kicked in and the screen broken. 'Oh Colin!' Julia began.

Then her attention was drawn to the wall over the boy's sagging and unmade bed. She gasped, and only prevented herself from running out into the sanity of sunlight by clutching at the sick creature she was now determined to save. Colin mouthed and gesticulated with pleasure as he saw Julia's eyes on the poster, larger than life, which hung on the wall over his bed.

Diana, Princess of Wales, dominated the foul-smelling little room in tiara and ball dress, her golden hair perfectly arranged, her lovely face set in an unending smile. The shepherd's son, choking with delight as Julia stood staring at the picture, dropped onto the bed and gurgled his love for his idol.

A knock at the door broke the silence between the woman at whom no one ever looked, and the boy people pretended not to see. A third presence, that of the woman the public longed above all to see again, became the most powerful in the room. The knocking continued, and a man's voice, semi-insolent, cautious, overlaid with a conscious charm, sounded through the walls of the small building.

'May I come in, please?' said David Baron.

CHAPTER SIX

The jeep lurched from side to side on the unmade road leading back down the glen to the castle. Julia, her eyes on the ditches either side – Baron drove with an aggression it would have been hard to guess at, from the generally obsequious and soft-throated courtierly air he gave off – prayed that the journey would come to an end soon. The shepherd's cottage in its verdant dip was left behind, and the track grew rougher as they began the climb uphill before turning into a part of the estate especially loved by the Prince of Wales, when he wanted to meditate in solitude: there were soft round hills here, each covered in heather at this time of year and resembling exotic dumplings, Julia thought. The wide burn which flowed through here, she knew, had proved a background for an unexpectedly successful photo shoot at the time of the Prince's engagement to the nineteen-year-old from an aristocratic family – everyone had fond memories of the picture of the plump, smiling face, the eager eyes and brown hair as yet untouched by a smart coiffeur. Julia sighed as they passed the outcrop of rock above the deep pool where salmon lay, ready to be caught by a royal fisherman. Nineteen years old… that was Harry's age now, went Julia's thoughts: how long ago that seemed, and how much had changed since then, both in the monarchy and the country as a whole!

As Baron jammed his foot on the brake to avoid a covey of partridges reared for the royal house-party, Julia closed her eyes, picturing the clear October days, the striding, tweeded figures, the pop-pop of the guns. Could their way of life continue indefinitely? It was hard to see. These reflections, coupled with the wild swaying of the jeep, kept Julia from acknowledging to herself that the driver, equerry and friend to the Prince of Wales, decidedly did not have his eyes on the road. He glanced continually at his passenger – the nurse Harry had said was his new friend: he'd announced he would beg his father to keep her on in some capacity after he had recovered, but there had been some doubts expressed over this – and each time his gaze settled on her, Julia felt a blush of annoyance rise in her cheeks. David Baron had been dismissive in the extreme at the shepherd's house, showing with barely concealed scorn what he thought of the wretched Colin, and expressing with a raised eyebrow and glacial tone his disapproval of the strange woman who had trespassed on the estate and walked into an employee's home. When Julia had explained who she was, his attitude had barely improved: it was as if, Julia thought in some agitation, she had been described and discussed before he had even met her. Was she so disliked, then? – of course, the answer came back to her, Mrs MacDuff the housekeeper had taken against her from the start and had probably spoken ill of her to the equerry. If it hadn't been for Baron's insistence on returning her to the castle in the jeep, she would have escaped and continued with her walk up the valley to the loch, a favourite picnic spot for royal children, which lay in the deep folds of the hills at the glen's end. It was tranquil there; she needed to rest and think after the morning's meetings in the sickroom; and if David Baron hadn't made it clear there was no alternative, she would have found solace in her planned loneliness.

But Baron knew just how to steer an unwanted spectator away from a royal Personage – and it was just this skill which enabled him to hustle Julia across the humpbacked bridge and into the jeep. Colin stood desolate in the doorway as they left.

The jeep turned sharply into a long avenue of tall trees and Baron accelerated, coming to a screeching halt as a figure ran out from a building at the end of the avenue. This was a stone replica of a Greek temple, placed in order to provide a vista for Queen Victoria and her numerous children, over a hundred years before. It contained a slatted wooden seat which ran around the inside walls – and there was just time to observe, before the woman darted into the centre of the road and waved Baron's vehicle down, that she had been sitting there, back against the wall, with a brown leather bag beside her on the seat.

Now this was waved frantically – and Julia, thrown forward against her seatbelt, was just able to recognise that this was a very expensive bag indeed before its owner, apparently not taking note of Julia at all, pulled open the jeep's rear door and climbed in. 'Thank goodness you came just in time,' Julia heard enunciated in a charming, low voice from just behind her head. 'David, I lost something in the to-ing and fro-ing this morning... I thought I'd ask MacDuff or Tibbie if they'd found it... I won't come in, y'know... now I've had the good luck to find you here. Can I tell you what it is?' – and then, noticing Julia – or so it appeared – for the first time – in the front passenger seat, 'Oh never mind... I'll tell you later...'

Julia's last five minutes of the drive back to Balmoral from the emptiness and innocence of the deserted glen were as uncomfortable to her heart and mind as the effect of the stones in the rutted surface of the avenue, on the royal jeep. Here, just a few inches behind her, sat the woman the world knew as the love of Charles's life: his companion, lover and friend. Here, smiling and composed – if the composure was ruffled by the temporary loss of some possession or other in the move from castle to lodge, there were only minimal signs of it – was the woman Charles might crown the next Queen of England, whether his subjects liked it or not. That it may have been unpleasant and snubbing, to receive the recent intimation they should move out (for what else could it have been? the Queen and the Duke of Edinburgh had attempted, perhaps, to halt the announcement of a marriage between their son and his mistress and had come up against a blank refusal to wait) did not show on the charming features of Mrs Parker Bowles. She seemed the type to deal with crises or lapses in good manners, or the misplacing of a cherished object – with good humour and equanimity. And now, as if to make up for ignoring the dowdily dressed nurse in the front seat, she leaned right forward and smiled charmingly. 'Good morning'. A waft of *Mitsouko* by Guerlain arrived in Julia's nostrils, and she edged away – for she knew and loathed the fragrance. 'Do tell me how dear Harry is today? – there were too many in there earlier to get a good idea...'

Too many, thought Julia. Yes, Camilla was known to like intimate meetings, confidential exchanges. 'His Royal Highness continues to make good progress,' Julia said, but with difficulty, as the jeep entered the courtyard of the royal stables and came to a halt. Then she found herself invisible again, as the soft-voiced appealing approach of the future consort of the King focused on his aide and equerry: 'If you're not coming in,' said Baron – and Julia felt the complicity between them as he spoke – 'then I'll pop in and ask MacDuff myself.'

'Oh thank you, David,' came the well-modulated tones.

Julia freed herself – as she was ever after to think of it – from her perfumed prison, and walked as quickly as she could without actually breaking into a run, from the stables entrance to the castle to the side door. She needed to see Harry – she had been away from him over an hour – and she felt his need for her, however much he might protest that she fussed over him too much and he preferred to be left alone. She turned once to look back at the jeep as she rounded the corner and walked over cobbles onto the smooth tarmac drive; and she saw Camilla, who had moved now to the seat Julia had just vacated. A cloud of blonde hair and a faint glow of pearls at the neck were visible through the windscreen. Julia squared her shoulders and walked on.

The White and Gold Room, bright in the sunshine an hour or so before, was sombre now, as storm clouds gathered from the west and hung over Deeside. It was ever the first part of the castle to reflect coming weather, Julia reflected as she knocked lightly at the door and waited for Harry's sweet command that she come in. The west wing of Balmoral could be counted on to run a full range of cinematic effects across the wide bay windows of the bedrooms apportioned to favoured guests; violent thunderstorms provided a show more dramatic than the end-of-summer fireworks, at the annual post-Braemar Games ball. And the haar, the thick Scottish mist – when it rolled in over the mountains, it gave Harry's sickroom the air of being cut off from the rest of the world: a spaceship floating in a sea of grey-white wool.

'Julia! Where have you been?' her young patient demanded. 'I'm stuck in this –' and he waved his computer game, despatched from London two days ago and at present taking up all his attention. 'What do I do now?' – and then, 'Oh hell!' as his bedside light, necessary now a rainstorm seemed increasingly likely, went out. 'It can't be the bulb,' Harry observed. 'John brought up a new one yesterday.'

'Dud, perhaps?' Julia suggested. She felt already a hundred times better than even a bare quarter of an hour before, as the memory of the drive back down the valley faded and Harry's delightful nature, both playful and serious, captivated her as it invariably did. The boy had an artistic temperament, in some ways, Julia thought, but didn't suffer from the tantrums and mood swings that so often go with it. If he had a fault, it was exuberance: sometimes he over-enjoyed himself, as Julia knew, and committed mistakes, silly pranks which could only lead him into trouble. But he was young – he would grow out of it – and the world would be a better place anyway if people let themselves go more. (So it would be hard not to think if you grew up in the tightly controlled atmosphere insisted on by the Royal Household.) 'The power's off,' announced the second in line to the throne, after pressing the On button on the TV remote: a black screen lowered at the occupants of the White and Gold Room, closely resembling the angry skies outside. 'I don't think that's ever happened in my lifetime,' the Prince added thoughtfully.

Julia was on her feet and testing the light switches in the passage outside the room before Harry had finished his sentence. She knew (for she knew the thoughts of her charge as if they were her own) that they both examined, without disclosing to the other, the possibility of a terrorist attack on Balmoral; and had decided, both, that the sudden darkness was very probably the result of a failure in the national grid rather than the actions of those repaying in kind the inhumanity of the recent Gulf War. But the castle could be seen as a 'soft target', Julia knew: security was hard to enforce here, in so rambling and huge a building. And the fact of the Queen's early arrival coupled with that of her son had in all probability taken the police off guard.

The first dazzling lightning, forked against the almost-invisible mountains, frightened Julia all the same. In the livid whiteness she looked across at Harry – and saw to her relief that he took the display as an enormous joke: she saw him laugh, red hair standing up on his head as if fire had darted in and struck him there in his bed. Then, a moment later as thunder began its drum roll above the turrets of the castle, she felt a sudden dejection from the same quarter and moved closer, to comfort the lad. He'd had enough, really, without the alarm a plunge into night at midday could provide. Hardly recovered from a life-defying fall, limbs broken and only slowly mending, the young Prince had been through too much for his years already. Even the possibility of an attack by suicide bombers determined to blow the Royal Family off the face of the earth, would seriously endanger his chances of getting better quickly.

'Never mind, Harry,' Julia whispered, cradling the fiery head in her arms as she might have done if he'd been ten years younger and struggling to conceal fear and apprehension at the ghosts of the coming night. 'We'll go for our little trip very soon, I promise. Now, where would you like to go? Up the valley to the loch, and we'll take our tea? Or we'll go into Ballater and maybe have a drink at the Stuart Arms – what would you feel about that?'

Harry remained silent, and as the next deafening onslaught from the crashing black clouds above filled the upper reaches of the castle, Julia fought her own anxiety that the power cut might in itself enable terrorists to enter Balmoral and wreak havoc in the heart of the sovereign's demesne. This would be a perfect time for them: she remembered the list in the housekeeper's room – summoned by Mrs MacDuff and interrogated about the loss of a pillowcase from the Prince's room, she had had to stand there while the housekeeper ostentatiously finished a letter, placed it in an envelope, and attached the monarch's head, second class – and the list had consisted of arrival dates of guests at the castle. She remembered, too, that Janet MacDuff had caught her staring down at it and absorbing the information that the Prime Minister was due imminently at Balmoral. A council meeting was required, to do with a strike against petrol prices – something of the sort. Julia had not been long enough back in the country to understand what the politics of his coming must be.

Another roar from thunder sounded horribly like an explosion of dynamite and Harry, eager still to maintain the sense of hilarity of it all, pushed Julia away from him. 'Get under the bed, Julia – no, I mean it. We used to play hide-and-seek in here sometimes – it was good fun. Go on, duck down there!'

Julia knew when Harry's voice broke a little that he remembered his childhood happiness, and her heart bled for him at these times. So, without demur, she dropped to her knees in the darkened sickroom and crawled under the bed, Harry's satisfied laughter followed her there.

Something square and hard pierced Julia's knee. She pulled herself painfully on her elbows away from the object, and brought it up to her eyes. Even the gloom down here couldn't dispel the knowledge of what she now held in her hands.

The ring... the blue ring. As a blaze of light suddenly illumined the room, she slipped it on her finger and crawled out. Of all things, what could this be doing here?

Janet MacDuff, Head Housekeeper at Balmoral, entered the room – the door was open and this was no time to knock and ask for admittance. 'There is a report of a missing item, property of Mrs Parker Bowles,' Mrs MacDuff announced.

'What on earth do you mean, Duffy?' demanded the young Prince from his bed.

'Yes,' came the voice of David Baron, breathless from his rapid climb up the castle to the west wing landing. 'It's more than likely that it was lost in here – you tell me her own room had been thoroughly searched'.

'Oh yes, certainly,' Mrs MacDuff said. Then she fell silent. Julia, who had reached a standing position at last, bent down to shake dust from her skirt. The ring slipped from her finger and clattered onto the floor. Two thoughts, both irrelevant, flitted through her mind as she turned to face the housekeeper – one, that wee Mary would get a drubbing for leaving the floor under Prince Harry's bed dirty, and the other was that the sapphire ring must have been widened, to accommodate another finger than her own.

'I'll have that please,' said David Baron, as he stooped to retrieve the ring.

'Come with me, Julia,' followed on Mrs MacDuff. She took the nurse's arm and led her from the room.

CHAPTER SEVEN

Before ten minutes had passed, Mrs MacDuff's small sitting room had filled up with people – staff members, two plain-clothes policemen still at the castle following the power cut earlier, and, kilted and on his way to a ceremony at the little local school this afternoon, the Chief of the Aberdeenshire Constabulary, Colonel Merriweather. Summoned by the Head Housekeeper, the crowd looked politely away from Julia as she faced MacDuff, her chief inquisitor across the highly polished table. No one looked, either, at the blue ring, which lay, as if about to be presented at a wedding or coronation to its rightful owner, on a square of black velvet Mrs MacDuff might have known would come in handy one day for this purpose. Eyes were averted from the nurse found crawling from under a royal bed, sporting the historic jewel. No one said, or even whispered, either blame or accusation. But if people glanced anywhere, it was in the direction of David Baron, the equerry, who occupied pride of place, his back to the mantelpiece and careful not to dislodge the photos and children's drawings of years long past, Christmas cards and expressions of esteem from the Royal Family.

Julia, in turn, could see, whether she liked it or not, little but herself. Mrs MacDuff's mirror, highly prized and daily dusted, hung behind the desk on the wall. It showed a flushed and flustered woman in a russet blouse and sensible skirt; the merest hint of a scar that ran from under neatly combed brown hair down over her cheekbone to her neck on the left hand side, and crossed over in the reflection to show itself on the right; and eyes, large, brown and startled, which gazed at the assorted members of an impromptu jury with more in them of defiance than of shame. Julia was tall – though, as Baron had noted when she descended from the jeep earlier that she suffered from a slight limp demonstrating that she had perhaps once been even taller – and the elaborate summit of the mirror, a diadem of art nouveau frosted glass, cut off the top of her head. To one side and at the rear, those involved in the alleged theft of the royal sapphire gathered, most of them shorter than the accused.

'You say, Sister Julia, that you went under the bed in His Royal Highness's room in order to play hide-and-seek,' Mrs MacDuff intoned. She was used to this kind of thing: a year or so back, with a large tea party at the castle under way and small children of royal or noble descent dressed up for the occasion, an album of the Queen's photographs had disappeared. It was thought to contain 'informal' shots of various family members, some of these taken in the now burnt-down beach hut near Sandringham, their usual venue for Hogmanay. The sale of pictures of what was rumoured to be an extremely informal barbecue – the sovereign had been confined to bed with a cold at the house and had not attended – would have been embarrassing in the extreme. Mrs MacDuff had ensured the nannies were interrogated in turn – Merriweather had overseen the procedure – and a young nanny had been taken to Aberdeen for further questioning. She had been found guilty and sentenced accordingly. Now it was Merriweather's turn to make short shrift of the Prince's nurse: he would ask his subordinates to drive 'Sister Julia' to the police station and would come himself to continue his interrogation once the school prize-giving was over. Already, in a hushed voice in the corridor, MacDuff had expressed her concerns over this person brought from the East and nothing at all known about her. What better way, the Head Housekeeper had hissed to Merriweather, could there be for an international crime ring than to penetrate Balmoral – or any of the royal palaces for that matter – and remove priceless jewellery and works of art? Look at His Grace the Duke of Buccleuch, just recently robbed of his Leonardo by a couple pretending to be sightseers at his home.

'It is hardly usual,' Merriweather said with heavy sarcasm, 'to play hide-and-seek alone. His Royal Highness, due to having to remain in bed, was able neither to hide nor to seek, I assume?'

The suppressed ripple of laughter expected by the Chief Constable

ran round the small sitting room. No one would show themselves
openly enjoying Merriweather's wit – but those who appreciated it
were repaid in various ways. 'So, Sister, you chose to hide just at the
time of the blackout – due to the falling of a branch on the line in the
unseasonably high winds we have been experiencing.'

David Baron leaned another quarter of an inch back against the
laden mantelpiece and concealed a small smile. A black-and-white
studio portrait of Prince Charles at the age of seven fluttered to the
ground and Mrs MacDuff, frowning, elbowed her way to retrieve it
from the floor. It was a piece of good luck that the mystery nurse, as
Baron thought of her, had been caught red-handed like this. She'd
have to go – whether it caused grief in some high places or not. And
now the housekeeper was standing next to him, fiddling with her
arrangement of mementoes, he was able to catch her eye and give her
a brief nod. Duffy'd be glad to see the woman out of the place too, he
knew. There was something not quite right with the set-up, altogether.
And now she'd proved herself to be a thief! 'Sister Julia was in the
jeep this morning with me,' Baron said. 'On the way down from the
Lodge, I picked up Mrs P-B and gave her a lift back here. She spoke of
having lost a valuable at the castle and Sister Julia would certainly have
heard her say it,' Baron continued. He was aware as he spoke of the
nurse's eyes turned on him, and for a moment he thought of a roe deer
he had shot on the neighbouring estate, a year back. Lord Beaucroft,
despite the ban, went ahead with hunting of both fox and stag – but
now, Baron thought with irritation, it would take some time before he
could enjoy the sport again, without thinking of those huge, reproach-
ful eyes. The truth was, the sooner this 'perfect carer' picked up in an
aid camp in Pakistan left the castle, the better. Tonight wouldn't be too
soon, as far as Baron was concerned.

'What do you have to say to this, Sister Julia?' Chief Constable
Merriweather said. 'It appears you knew the ring was missing and you
went to the White and Gold Room with that knowledge. You then
took advantage of the power cut.'

'I didn't know what was under the bed,' Julia said, her voice so low
that wee Mary, standing on tiptoe to hear, said afterwards that she'd
come over faint like the time she saw a ghost outside on the lawn,
walking towards the library door. It was getting right up close to Sister

Julia that had surprised her – but she couldn't say quite how or why. 'My hand brushed against it in the dark,' Julia said. 'That's all.'

'So you slipped it on your finger,' Mrs MacDuff said drily. 'Exactly so.'

'Excuse me.' John, the Head Footman, pushed his way to the front of the desk. 'We have an inaccuracy here, Colonel. Sister Julia cannot have known the position of the jewel. She had left the Prince's sick-room by the time it fell under the bed. I am in no doubt about it.'

All eyes turned on John as he related in minute detail the comings and goings of the morning. He had indeed seen the blue stone on the finger of its owner, while Julia had slipped from the room to ask the doctor to supply another prescription for her patient. It was then, surely, that the sapphire must have slipped and rolled under the bed. 'I went out into the corridor to find Sister Julia coming towards me with a slip of paper,' John concluded. 'She asked me to see to it that the prescription was filled as soon as possible. Sister Julia could not have been present when the ring fell under the bed.'

David Baron was to think later that what he would remember most of this morning's scene of accusation of the nurse was the way those eyes changed their expression: darkening as she was vindicated by the careful, plodding John; shining through tears as Colonel Merri-weather, reluctantly accepting the evidence, refused to go so far as to produce an apology. And finally, triumphantly blazing as the sitting room emptied, and, with one backward glance, Sister Julia left herself to continue with her duties. Baron and Mrs MacDuff were left alone. An uncomfortable silence fell.

'Well, I don't know,' Mrs MacDuff said. 'It's funny, but – '

'Impossible,' David Baron said.

CHAPTER EIGHT

Julia left Mrs MacDuff's room and walked without thought of direction down dark passages and across crepuscular landings, all these part of the servants' wing of the great castle. From some rooms (all doors were firmly closed) came the muffled sound of sewing machines or the muted roar of vacuum cleaners; from others the sudden sweet and sickening smell of drying clothes, hung on long heated pipes installed in Victorian times. Invisibly, carefully, the summer of the Royal Family was nurtured, preserved and made ready for enjoyment and duty here.

Flights of stairs covered in the harsh grey cord deemed suitable to walk on for those who sewed, patched, mended, polished, scrubbed and dusted, led downwards and, still without apparent consciousness of where she went, Julia followed them into the depths of the building. Here were what seemed to be miles of red tiles underfoot, met dizzyingly by walls clad in institutional white tiling. Doors, some at least, were ajar and revealed stillrooms where jams and jellies stood neatly labelled on shelves. Others formed a dairy, with butter pats laid clean on great wooden tables, ready to impress the royal crest, while new butter, in lumps of a milky yellow white, sat in muslin cloths. A telephone room, labelled as such, led directly off the main subterranean corridor. Its door opened beneath the rows of brass bells, these gleaming and still clearly in use, which summoned servants to the rooms upstairs. As Julia stood gazing up at them, a bell rang with a tinny, imperious note: the Queen's boudoir, Julia saw, required immediate attention. Then another bell jangled: the Lavender Room, high on the VIPs' landing,

43

announced the arrival and now-declared needs of distinguished guests. It was as if the wires tugging at their brass mouthpieces set the whole system in motion: the Queen in her counting house, counting out her money, the servants preparing the bread and honey down below. And woe betide any member of the serving class caught appropriating some of the wealth of those bell-ringers upstairs: Julia's cheeks still burned at the thought of Mrs MacDuff's hard eyes, the Chief Constable's complacency – and, worst of all, the infinite contempt and suspicion in the manner of the Prince's equerry David Baron. She, whose love and care for young Harry had been praised by his grandmother and recognised by his father, had been treated like a shop girl found with her hand in the till. Now, as never before, Julia ached to leave Balmoral and return to her life of caring for the poor and ill halfway across the world.

'I thought you came out of all that very well,' a voice said. 'Guilty without proof, that's how they seem to want it here.'

Julia turned, and saw John the Head Footman. The red and white tiles of the passage rose and fell around him, as she fought to control her tears: it was a fatal mistake, she knew, to show anything of your true feelings in this place. She hadn't heard him coming because she struggled with a heart that beat so fast it blocked out the sound of footsteps. 'You know,' John said, 'there are too many here who wish for the old way of life to go on as before –'

Julia found herself nodding in agreement as John spread out his hands palm upwards, as if in resignation and despair. She looked at him more closely as he spoke, and realised the pale, almost colourless face and quiet eyes were those of a man who had the courage to speak his mind – though in performing his duties she had never found him other than an ideal servant, thus without opinions of his own. 'She made all the difference here,' John said. 'Balmoral became another place. Young – full of life and possibilities. Now it's a museum again. And they don't admit to what she did for them – they didn't like her then and they hide away from thinking of her now.'

Julia felt herself blush – then the colour drained from her face and she leant against the hard white tiles beneath the row of bells. One went off as she stood there: the Library wanted immediate response to a guest or royal incumbent's needs. The bell jangled on and then stopped, as if aware that no one had any desire to obey. 'I loved her,'

John said. He spoke without emotion, his eyes trained on the floor as so often when serving the great silver platters of game he took round a table of twenty, back and arms bending under the weight, the necessity of placing the feet in an exactly right position for the distinguished guest to take the food causing him to stare always down. Now, Julia saw, John was free; perhaps his holding his hands out empty was a sign of his liberation from his duties; he looked straight at her at last and, thinking this, she found herself smiling at him with a sense of real affection. 'They couldn't understand her, you know,' John said. Then, as silence fell between them, he pulled a key from the bunch which hung just inside the telephone room and waved it in Julia's face. 'Come and see her clothes, sister,' he said. 'I know you'll like to see them – MacDuff locked them away down here and they're mostly the dresses she wore when she was engaged or just married, all the grand stuff went on show elsewhere. The shoes, too.'

'The shoes?' Julia said faintly, as Mrs MacDuff's voice came in a roar from two floors above, demanding to know why no one answered the bells. 'Why – where are all – her things, then?'

John took Julia's arm and guided her through the telephone room and into a passage leading to a door marked Turret Entrance: Private.

'They're in here,' John said, as a tintinnabulation of bells broke out from the corridor behind them.

The rooms which opened out once John had undone the double lock on the mysteriously named Turret Entrance were, Julia saw, arranged with an almost obsessive regard for order. Long rails of dresses, coats, two-piece suits, ball dresses and informal wear stood in formation, their bagged contents resembling passengers on a stationary train. At the sides of the rooms, three in all, which succeeded each other in this never-visited part of the castle, were stacked shelves of shoes, equally guarded by soft leather or cotton shoe bags, and long tubes, these filled with tissue paper, containing elbow-length and wrist-length gloves. Being in a semi-basement, a near-darkness filled this memorial to the departed Princess, but the rooms were occasionally lit by a shaft of sun from the bright day in the gardens outside. Grass, trimmed by zealous gardeners, pressed against the windows halfway up, giving an air of an undug or premature grave. Julia turned to John – and this time there was no concealing the emotion which overcame her and rendered her, for a minute or so, unable to speak.

'It's all done by MacDuff,' John said in the precise, neutral tones used to reply to royal queries or commands. ('I wouldn't know, sir' – Julia had heard him answer his masters in this way, and had reflected that the Head Footman must often know, but if the question had a thorny side to it, then he'd find he shouldn't, rather than wouldn't tell the truth.) Trouble came to those who knew too much, in a household such as this; and now John, who pretended not to observe the nurse's extreme reaction to this shrine – for despite the housekeeper's intentions the collection amounted to a powerful memory of a much-mourned member of the Royal Family – walked tactfully through into the last of the three rooms and waited for Julia to regain her calm.

This was a time, Julia was to think later, that she needed desperately then and not only for the finding of her usual composure. It was a time that seemed, as she went slowly and hesitantly at first from rail to rail, pulling at calico shrouds or lightly running a zip down the side of a container holding a long-forgotten ball dress, to encompass a multitude of other times: youth and its hopes and expectations; times of music and dancing; tears and solitude, in the despair of first unhappiness. What was this dress, its pinkness, its silky skirt printed with green flowers writhing on the expensive fabric? How had its wearer survived the jealousy and anger of the evenings when to fail to smile in public was to be reprimanded, and to be seen to weep obscene? How could these rows of long-unworn clothes, each marking a formal occasion or a private grief, appear to hold a power still over those who saw them?

'It was I who persuaded MacDuff to put this on its own,' John said from the next room as Julia, pausing by the shelves of shoes, half-pulled a strappy sandal from its suede bag. 'She didn't want to at first – but I said that one day when this collection goes on show, she'd be admired for her decision to select the dress that made the world love the beautiful young woman who danced with her devoted husband –'

John stopped, and Julia knew as she went through into the third chamber, that he was aware already of having said too much. For a moment, she wished to flee the unintended sanctum – but how could she fail to please John, now? He had saved her, after all, from the ignominy of arrest at the hands of the police – and from expulsion from

Balmoral. The probability that she would never have seen her young patient again made her shudder. 'I'm coming,' Julia said; and it was only as she went through into a room darker than the others and lit, as she now saw, by a single spotlight, that she realised she held the black patent sandal in her hand.

'Come and stand over here and look,' John said. His voice was no longer that of an anonymous staff member, but strong and filled with pride and affection. 'The diamonds aren't real, of course – I brought these costume rocks up from London – but they give an idea of that magical evening.'

The dress, a ball dress with plunging neckline and wide organza skirt, was black, the midnight hue enhancing the paleness of the shop mannequin inside it; and somehow, perhaps by reason of the yellow curled wig and perfect, figure-hugging cut of the swirling folds, it appeared to give an almost life-like air to its wearer. The face was not unlike its one-time owner – it could have been modelled on the original, Julia thought. But then, the nose was demonstrably not a recognisable copy: it was short and tilted, as noses of shop mannequins invariably were. Standing beside John in the flood of spotlight as he murmured about the palpable romance between the Prince and his young wife in Canada all those years ago, which had seized the attention – and then gained the love and admiration – of millions, Julia could only stare up in silence at this artificial princess.

'We'll be wanted upstairs,' John said as a chorus of bells sounded along the passages of the castle basement. 'Why Arthur's not down here to see to all this I don't know. Back to the treadmill.' And he smiled, while Julia, unable to answer him, went slowly through into the first rooms of Mrs MacDuff's arrangement of royal outfits. 'Now you don't want to take that shoe with you,' John chided his new friend. And, laughing: 'It's a Manolo, sister – already a museum piece. At least take them both while you're about it.'

But Julia could only mutter something about going up to the sickroom to be with her patient. He would need reassuring – that she was still here to care for him – that she hadn't vanished as suddenly as she had come. 'I'll make sure he gets to the picnic up at the loch tomorrow,' Julia said more to herself than to John as he unlocked the door marked Turret Private Entrance and ushered her through. 'See you later,' John called after her. But the nurse had disappeared down the passage in the direction of the staircase up into the main block of the castle, before he could say any more.

CHAPTER NINE

Picnics at Balmoral were keenly anticipated by some, a challenge to others. For some of the staff, assembling the food and equipment for the picnic was a welcome change from the normal routine, for others, such as Mrs MacDuff, an exercise in perfection which, like all such exercises, could be ruined by unpredictable forces, in this case, the weather. Guests, too, were often in two minds about the picnics. Not everyone was comfortable with the formal informality of the occasions. Not everybody enjoys eating outside wearing tweeds and sweaters.

David Baron was on the whole unenthusiastic about the Balmoral picnics. He was not easy with picnic etiquette and he preferred to keep his clothes away from contact with the ground, grass, bushes and, especially, mud. However, when he got up early on the morning following the extraordinary crisis concerning Mrs Parker Bowles's ring, he was encouraged to see, from the windows of his bedroom at the Lodge, sunshine and clear skies. He was not on duty that morning although he would be expected at the picnic later. He quickly showered and dressed and left the Lodge quietly – it was too early for the staff to be about although he heard a radio playing softly, in the kitchen.

He drove to the castle and parked to one side of the drive, under a tree, keeping his eyes on the massive doors. There was a detective outside, who had acknowledged his presence without interest. Baron sat and waited.

On the brief drive to Balmoral, breakfastless, he had questioned himself about whether it was really worth giving up a free morning to watch out for Sister Julia, who was probably, now, just getting up and preparing to go to the sickroom. He and the housekeeper both suspected her of something, although they weren't sure what it was. But even if there was some secret, or some hidden agenda behind Julia's presence at the palace, it wasn't part of his responsibility to find out what it was. He was part of the Prince's household, not the Queen's. And yet, he now knew, he couldn't leave the problem alone.

His eyes still on the front door he suddenly remembered the brief glance Julia had cast at him in the housekeeper's room, as she was undergoing investigation concerning the ring. Her submissive, doe-like brown eyes had met his smooth courtier's mask. What had he seen in that glance? She was unsettled, of course, because of what was happening and yet, beneath the uncertainty, he had felt an unusual strength. How had she come by that confidence? A palace is a place where everyone is to an extent dependent – servants and courtiers need the approval of those they serve, while guests, except for those of the inner circle, are very conscious of the privilege of staying there, in a royal palace, as guests of the sovereign. Julia's manner suggested she did not seek approval.

Baron's philosophy of life was a simple one. He believed that everybody wanted something and once you knew what it was you had the key to them, and a way of predicting what they were likely to do. Reared in a vicarage he understood that some people were motivated by other desires than the obvious – money, love, status, power, respectability. They might want God, to do their duty, freedom from sin. But Baron could not fit Julia into any of the categories he knew – not the worldly one, nor into the ranks of the pious or the conscience-ridden members of his father's congregation. Baron couldn't work out what Julia wanted, and it upset him. Mrs MacDuff said she knew her way about the castle – and the business with the dog – what the hell was all that about? Baron smelt danger, which to him meant danger to himself, his career, his well-being.

He decided he didn't understand Julia, and also, without knowing why, he just didn't like her. Whether it made sense or not, he'd go on watching. As for this particular mission, he'd give it an hour and then, if nothing happened, return to the Lodge and tell everyone he'd gone for an early drive as it was such a lovely day.

And then Julia came out, exchanged a word with the detective on the steps and walked off towards the garages. It was just seven o'clock and she was going for a drive. Why? Minutes later she was back at the wheel of the off-road vehicle which had been specially converted for Prince Harry. She pulled up at the steps and the maid, Mary, promptly appeared in the doorway with Prince Harry, in his wheelchair. Julia lowered the ramps at the back. The detective and the maid began to get the wheelchair down the steps with Prince Harry smiling and looking round at the world he had seen too little of over the past weeks. As they went through the tricky business of moving the wheelchair down to the ground and then up the ramp at the back of the vehicle, Baron put his car in gear and slid it round the corner in the direction of the garages. Once out of sight he took a back road, was waved through the gates by the policeman on duty and drove a little way up the main road which led past the castle. There he parked – and waited. He had no idea whether Julia would be using the road but he knew that, if she were just taking Prince Harry for a drive to some favourite spot on the estate he could not follow. He would be too obvious on those empty roads.

Over half an hour later, just as he had concluded Julia had taken her patient to the river, or up on to the moor for some fresh air and a change of scene, he saw the vehicle turn into the road. Julia was driving and there was another figure beside her. She could not have got Prince Harry out of his wheelchair and into the front of the car. It would have been too risky, and too painful for him. So who was the other figure? Was Prince Harry even in the back of the car?

Baron followed at a safe distance. He thought he could see Prince Harry's bright hair in the back window. So he was still in the vehicle. But who was the other figure?

Prince Harry studied Julia's back as she drove, and her capable hands on the wheel. He called, from the wheelchair, 'How far is it?'

'Nearly a hundred miles,' she said. 'It'll take a couple of hours.'

He groaned in protest. 'Pipe down,' she told him. She turned to the figure beside her. 'Looking forward to it, Colin?' she asked.

'Not a lot,' he muttered. He was very pale. 'Thanks all the same,' he said. 'I don't know how you've managed it – there's a waiting list a mile long for rehab. They say you've usually OD'd by the time you get your place. How did you do it?'

'This isn't standard rehab,' Julia told him. 'This is luxury rehab. You're going to a country house set up to rehabilitate drug and alcohol abusers. Fairbairn Lodge. You'll have to mind your Ps and Qs there, I'm telling you.'

'What!' Colin cried. 'You've to pay to go there! We can't afford that. Turn round now! We've to go back.'

Julia drove on calmly. 'It's all paid,' she said. 'Don't worry – all you have to do is get better.'

Colin swung round to look at Prince Harry. 'Did you do this?' he accused.

'Nothing to do with me, mate,' he replied. 'This is all news to me. It's you, Julia, isn't it?'

Julia said nothing. Colin swore. 'It is you, isn't it, Julia? Why did you do that? Where would you get the money from – you're just a nurse.'

'I've spent the last few years in a refugee camp in Pakistan,' Julia said. 'They paid me but there was nothing to spend money on. So there we are.'

'You've no call to spend what you've got on a worthless tyke like me,' Colin said. 'I'm a disappointment. I've been a disappointment all my life – ask anybody. I'm not worth your money.'

'They'll fix that problem with your self-esteem while you're there,' Julia said placidly. 'Then – once you're clean – don't come back.'

'Don't come back?' Colin said.

'No – get a job – get some training – go to London – emigrate – you can do it. But don't come back.'

He turned round. 'What do you think, Harry?'

'Do what Julia says,' came a sober voice from the back of the car.

Baron continued to follow the vehicle containing Julia, the Prince and Colin through moorland landscape, through a small town and onward over a high, empty moorland road. Baron kept his distance on the near-empty roads. Then Julia, Baron still behind, dipped down on to a narrow tree-lined country road. After a mile, her car turned off, through a gateway. There were pillars with carved heraldic figures on either side. Baron drove past, observing a long drive with an imposing house at the end of it. He parked on the grass beside the road and ran quickly back. He sneaked a look up the drive and saw Colin, standing next to a man in a white coat, saw Julia give him a swift hug and then turn back to her car. Baron retreated and went to sit in his own vehicle. He saw, in the mirror, Julia drive away down the road. He waited, knowing there was no point in following. Julia would be taking Prince Harry back to Balmoral. They'd be just in time for the picnic.

He sat thinking for a moment. What was all that about? Julia had dragged Prince Harry on a long drive to take a worthless junkie to an expensive clinic. Was that all right? It certainly couldn't have been part of her job. Did the Queen know? Had someone had to pay? If so – who? It made no sense. He'd talk it over with Mrs MacDuff. He put his car in gear.

They were all late for the picnic due to an overturned lorry ten miles from Balmoral. Baron sat sweating in his car in a long queue of traffic, knowing, because he'd checked how long it had been since the accident, that Julia and Prince Harry were probably up ahead, nearer the head of the queue, but they were, all three of them, going to be late. And of course he knew that unpunctuality was, in royal circles, practically a hanging crime. No one was allowed to arrive later than the Queen or Prince Charles. Anyone other than a favourite such as himself would lose his job, or be humiliatingly demoted. The only consolation was that Julia would be out, neck and crop, for today's exploits.

CHAPTER TEN

It had rained on and off all morning, and two footmen were engaged in laying waterproof sheets under tartan rugs on the grassy slopes above the loch by the time Mrs MacDuff arrived, driven in the first of a fleet of Land Rovers by Tom Alves, the gamekeeper employed on the estate to collect and drop off the bag of the day in the Balmoral kitchens. The shots, ranged on the high hills that surrounded the large, triangular patch of black water that comprised Loch Adelaide (named after one of Victoria's daughters), were coming down, treading the burns and gullies of heathered land, and as they came the housekeeper, already twenty minutes behind schedule, tutted with exasperation at the sound of cascading pebbles and sharp bursts of gunfire accompanied by the thud of falling birds. It had been the unexpected arrival of Prince William that had done it, Mrs MacDuff repeated under her breath, and for her own benefit: she didn't like to sound a note of criticism about a royal to anyone other than David Baron, and the equerry had been inexplicably absent this morning. It had been almost impossible to decide where to put the young woman the Prince had brought with him, too: the Ivy Room, perhaps, where ladies could be visited through an adjoining dressing room, by their companions? – or the seldom-used first floor of the castle's west wing? Here were saucy aquatints and boudoir furnishings of a long-gone Edwardian age, when married women and their husbands, in the time of Edward VII, exchanged bedroom keys or spent the night with their chosen paramours without causing any embarrassment to either host or servants. The Queen, of course, didn't go for this kind of entertaining: if the rooms remained the same as a hundred years before, it was due to the monarch's basic sense of economy; and if Mrs MacDuff flinched sometimes on searching for dust in the frames of the Boucher nude or Rubens sketch, where wide thighs and rosy bosoms trembled as she adjusted the line of the picture, she reminded herself sternly that this must be endured for the sake of saving strain on the privy purse. No, Her Majesty would not approve of placing the girlfriend of the heir to the throne in what was commonly known as a past setting for adulterous couples. And the worst of it was, the housekeeper reflected grimly, that the young woman the Prince had brought with him had herself brought evidence of having been one half of a couple, wed or otherwise. The child, a boy of about seven, who had looked about him with wide eyes on arriving in the Great Hall at Balmoral, was undeniably her son. The Prince was fond of him, that was clear also. Where do you put a single mother-cum-girlfriend in a royal palace? – and where do you put the child?

Mrs MacDuff was mulling over these problems as she began, with the help of Tom Alves and one of the footmen, to unload the picnic. Slabs of a rough game pâté, chicken and pasta larded with smoked salmon, were handed in monogrammed (again Edwardian) boxes to the staff to place on a table set up by the side of the picnic site. The fact that wee Mary had neglected to put in the silver goblets for the sloe vodka – this considered an essential for rain-drenched and freezing guns back from four hours on the moor without refreshment – had Tom back in the Land Rover to dash to the castle to repair the omission. As he went, and whole hams in breadcrumbs along with Deeside salmon and mayonnaise were carried with care to the serving table, Mrs MacDuff saw a line of sporting vehicles come up the winding road towards the loch. For a moment it looked as if there wasn't room for Alves, home-bound, to pass them, and she sighed. It was one of those days. Even Harry, the most immobile of Balmoral's residents, had gone out early – 'to revisit a beauty spot or two' as that besom of a nurse had put it last night when they'd passed on the stairs – and there was still no sign of them being in time for the picnic. No one was where they should be, today; and when they did turn up, she had a hard time trying to know where to put them.

The rain started to pelt down in earnest just as the first battalion of guns rounded the grassy path that led down the lower slopes of the hill. John the Head Footman, disembarking from a jeep in the convoy newly arrived up the valley, signalled for the rugs to be picked up and folded away. The picnic would have to take place in the boathouse, where Victorian tables and chairs and dark pine-panelled walls gave an air of a snooker room in an old-fashioned film set. Shutters were drawn back with excruciating shrieks from unoiled hinges – it must be a year at least since the family had picnicked up here at Loch Adelaide. Mrs MacDuff felt a headache coming on.

It was said, later, when Baron's account to Mrs MacDuff of how he had followed the woman, apparently a self-appointed carer for Prince Harry and now, in his view, in urgent need of investigation, all the way to the Tweedsdale Estate and the large eighteenth-century house there which constituted the privately funded rehab centre, that the Royal Family was fortunate indeed to employ such a man as equerry and volunteer private detective. What right had this Sister Julia – her surname, when checked, turned out not to exist, an unforgivable lapse on the part of security: Sir Michael Vane would have to answer for this, down at Clarence House – what credentials did this unknown and possibly untrained nurse possess, that she should place the son of an employee on the estate into medical care? And take the second son of the Prince of Wales along as well! It was both incomprehensible and dangerous in the extreme. Was this dull-looking woman, past her thirties and perhaps a sufferer from some unpleasant affliction – why, after all, did she limp and what exactly had occasioned the seldom visible but undeniable distortion of her features – to be trusted with HRH on long drives into the Highlands? Why did she pay for the rehab of the shepherd's son – as Baron, in a phone call en route to the picnic, had discovered? Who *was* Sister Julia? – spectral women terrorists inserted themselves in the minds of those confided in by Mrs MacDuff after David Baron had unburdened himself to her on arrival at the picnic site. For assistance with the problem of catching out the suspicious nurse, a few confidantes would be chosen for their proximity to the young Prince and his attendant. They would be able to gauge what was going on and the housekeeper could act accordingly. John the Head Footman and the longest-serving of the Queen's female secretaries,

Miss Murray, would be asked to probe deeper into the past and present movements of Sister Julia. John took the royal tray for breakfast and lunch up to the White and Gold Room and would be asked to report on any new plans for outings aired by Harry's attendant, and presented as being beneficial to the boy in one way or another. Miss Murray, to whom the young Prince dictated letters of thanks in reply to condolences and enquiries from all over the world as a result of his accident, would be asked to look out for unusual correspondence, demands for air tickets and so on, which might come in if the nurse wished to kidnap her charge and demand a ransom from the Queen.

For the present, all that was known was that the recent cloudburst had delayed the royal party in their departure for the loch. David Baron, late himself, had secretly thanked the Scottish climate for permitting him to arrive before the sovereign and her newly-arrived guests, the Prime Minister and his wife: his story of trailing Harry and the nurse on a charitable expedition to a home for suffering addicts might have gone down badly if given as an excuse for the misdemeanour of appearing after the Queen or Prince of Wales at a function, however informal. In fact, as he reflected, he could not have offered it at all. And now, standing a moment with Mrs MacDuff as a surprisingly strong sun broke through the clouds and a bevy of attendants rushed the picnic from the boathouse outside again – Her Majesty had said she would like to have the barbecue today and Tom Alves was sent back and forth for tiny chops and strings of chipolatas to the castle – Baron confided further in the housekeeper he counted on as his chief ally at Balmoral. 'She seemed to know young Colin?' were the only words which escaped Mrs MacDuff's lips as the rest of the story of Sister Julia's morning journey and Baron's pursuit was relayed to her. And then, 'You say she *paid* herself, David? Now that is most unusual.' Baron assured her that a quick word on his mobile with the secretary at Fairbairn Lodge, a former employee at the castle, had assured him of that fact. 'So where is she now?' Mrs MacDuff demanded, as the convoy of royal cars grew nearer on the road up the valley. 'She dropped Prince Harry here just before you arrived – he's in the boathouse with his DVDs, bless him. Surely you'd have seen her – one of you would have had to reverse to let the other pass?' And Mrs MacDuff looked keenly for a moment at the flustered equerry as if she might decide to doubt the truth of what he had just told her.

Baron fell silent. He remembered, on his way up the glen, seeing a jeep, only its back half visible, parked halfway down a steep bank at the side of the burn. There was no one in the vehicle and he'd assumed – he now urgently wondered why – that Sam the water bailiff was doing something or other there. Harry loved to fish for the small brown trout that lived in the burn, and for all Baron knew, Sam was weeding the sides like he did with loch and pond when royal visitors came to enjoy a spot of fishing. Now, of course, he realised his mistake. 'Christ!' he muttered, as both he and the Head Housekeeper suffered visions of car bombs and flying limbs, all the fault of the unobservant equerry. Baron pulled out his mobile and began jabbing. 'The Queen and her party are way past the place where the jeep was left –' he began.

'Yes, wait a minute or two and then put out an alert to find that Sister Julia,' Mrs MacDuff said. 'It'll take the focus off you not having noticed the vehicle if there's a full scale alert. Thank God Harry is safely here,' she added. Baron knew the state of the housekeeper's alarm by her way of referring to the Prince – for, even with an intimate such as Baron, Mrs MacDuff would invariably refer to 'His Royal Highness, Prince Harry'. MacDuff must be rattled indeed – and with a reason, Baron thought grimly.

CHAPTER ELEVEN

Julia stood on the high point of the highest hill overlooking the loch and paused a moment to take in the panorama of cleuch, heather-covered slopes and, on the gentle inclines of the foothills, the forest of ancient Scots pine and larches known as the Burnwood. The sun had dispersed the clouds, as she climbed; and the famous triangle of black water that was the man-made loch created by King Edward VII for the pleasure of boating and flirting with ladies in their sailor outfits, glinted several hundred feet below. It was a perfect day; and if Julia extended her moment of apparent indecision, it was because she had no desire to turn her head further to the west. Here, the Lodge occupied by the present heir to the throne, sheltered in a deep cleft of rugged mountainside that was its sole protection from storms and prying eyes alike, sat white and simple as a shepherd's cottage, the luxurious conservatory extension and other quarters devoted to the comfort of the late King's guests invisible from the valley below. Yet it was this that Julia both wished and dreaded to see: the rattan chairs in the tropically-heated glass ballroom grouped round lacquered tables laden with magazines devoted to interiors and architecture; the palm trees brought from the Gulf Stream-fed coast of Scotland; the rich chestnut furnishings and cabinet with its display of bottles all came into her mind, the image floating there inescapably – but whether she, in turn, had lately seen a magazine feature of this very place or had known it in reality would have been impossible to say.

There were no two ways about it. She must go there, lose a hundred feet or so by slithering across a ravine and scrambling through a half-grown allotment of conifers, these heartily disliked by the Prince of Wales and a subject of many of the many minor arguments with his mother on the subject of the upkeep of the estate. She must keep to the valley side of the mountain, where the thin belt of windbreak trees would almost conceal her if she walked with care; she must arrive unseen and drink in the feel of the place, its solitude amongst the miles of surrounding land, its apparent welcome and its final rejection of any visitor who dared to believe they had the freedom to walk or ramble in the place. There was no security here, it was true; and it was probably the nearest to living like an ordinary human being that a member of the Royal Family could have, on this windswept height with only a rough track to connect it with the valley and the loch below. But the loch itself was a dead end: the mountains that rose above it went on into a far distance, impossible to navigate without expert help. This, the White Lodge as it was known, was the ultimate retreat.

Julia's neat skirt and white blouse were torn and her hair dishevelled by the time the narrow, treacherous path across the ravine had been walked across – and her hands bleeding from so often having to cling to small boulders above the line marked in small, agonisingly sharp stones. Yet she would go on: aware that she now resembled a trespasser rather than a tourist, and had herself crossed the line between one with apparent criminal intent and a mere rambler, she ran the last hundred yards or so downhill in the green bowl of uplands grass which held the Lodge. The morning lay behind her now, like the tricky terrain she had doubted she could cover, in her quest for one, possibly last look at this hidden abode; and the jeep and its journey up the glen only a few hours ago felt as distant as the peaks, still snow-covered on this late summer day, which reared up behind Balmoral's best-kept secret, the hideaway not even camera crews could discover from air or land. A memory of the drive, and the sweet invalid she had conveyed, did, it was true, return as she ran. She was here, so far from all she had vowed to give her life to, for his sake. Yet she knew this climb into the private life of another was wrong – and worse than wrong, for it could bring shame or even harm to her charge if she were to be found here. Her motives would be questioned; and she knew herself already to be under suspicion, though for no crime that could confidently be stated. Now, after this flash of realisation, she saw that the vehicle which had started the train of thought was probably already considered highly suspicious in itself. Checks would be made on the jeep, for explosives and concealed means of communication. It must look as if it had been abandoned for a reason, Julia thought, remembering the haste with which she had steered it down the bank beside the burn. And of course there had been a reason, if not the one that would be looked for: a reason from the heart, and not from the violent mind of a terrorist or assassin. It was simply that she had waited too long. After all these years and now after all the days and hours since her coming to the Highlands – with the young Prince safely in the boathouse, she could wait no more. Did she – could she – guess at what she might feel if, unknown and unexpected, she arrived in the place where privacy announced itself by absence of noise and surveillance came only from the rooks that flew in the high trees leading down to the Burnwood? As for *his* feelings on seeing her like this – she could not dare to believe they might equal hers.

It seemed as if, for the long stretch of a lifetime, there had been nothing – and now, unmistakably, suddenly, here she was. Julia's knees trembled, and she ceased her run as the cottage came into view. Before she could arm herself against her fear and excitement, the glass walls of the Edwardian conservatory were visible: a tangle of orchids and the bright orange blossoms of hibiscus were vivid against the backdrop of drear mountain seen on the far side of the room through ornate glass windows. She was here; and so, inside and sitting in those rattan armchairs of which she had dreamed on her long ascent from the valley, were a man and a woman. Them, unmistakably so. The woman smiled across at the man and picked up the coffee pot on the low table between them. She poured; the man nodded; and she handed the filled cup over to him. The comfort and contentment of the scene were almost palpable.

Julia stood staring. The ground surrounding the Lodge was steep and she steadied herself by hanging onto the branch of the great rhododendron bush which partly concealed her from view. But she knew herself to be in danger, and absurdly visible if either of this long-settled couple should look up and gaze from the glass-walled room where they sat. She knew she must leave now: she had seen what she had seen: but a new hunger possessed her, and she found herself sliding further down the bank rather than fighting to regain height and escape notice through the protecting pines and Scots firs. As she slid, the Prince looked up at last from his coffee – and away from the warm smile of his companion – and saw her there.

The police helicopter from Aberdeen churned the bright air above Loch Adelaide and headed west into the mountains. Miles below, the tiny figures of the Queen of the United Kingdom, her Prime Minister and members of her Court, gazed upwards in surprise at the chopper, scarlet and appearing to dance like a dragonfly as it flew over the great white ravine. The barbecue would not be interrupted, despite security advice that Her Majesty should return to the castle instantly. Things would go on as before, as they always had.

Julia ran along the sides of the conservatory and out onto the platform of land above the vertiginous descent into the Burnwood. Her footing was sure, now; the path, through mossy glades and trees so high they closed together before the blue sky could come between them, went over simple bridges, logs strapped together over the rushing burn beneath. As she ran, down and down, the helicopter grew fainter, and soon could not be heard, over the sound of the waterfall in the centre of the wood. She ran on across it, and down the final, wider path out onto the hill above the loch, and the royal party.

CHAPTER TWELVE

The Queen was standing by the barbecue when the ill-kempt figure of 'Sister Julia' emerged from a belt of larches on the hillside. Known to the Queen as her grandson's carer – but, unusually for a monarch who famously never forgot a face, barely recognised on the occasions, generally on the landing outside Harry's sickroom, when they came up against each other – the nurse was little more than an anonymous member of staff at Balmoral. Now, with her startling appearance at the edge of a band of straggling trees, and the relevance of the positioning of the police helicopter directly above, there could be no mistaking the dowdy Julia, and no doubt that the speed at which she ran, coupled with the expression of horror on her face, signalled some recent act of desperation. Why, oh why, the Queen wondered, had the young Prince been permitted to bring this unstable stranger into the family? What damage had she done already, in her trespassing of the royal estate? The Queen, not one to show panic, speared a wild boar sausage, made from the latest trophy of a day's hunting on the neighbouring Beauclerk acres. This was a speciality made with spices and high-grade breadcrumbs by Mrs Hepburn, supervisor of the Balmoral kitchens. It would not do to look too closely at the woman who now, on seeing the royal party, made efforts to control the ungainly way she ran down the last stretch of slope towards the loch. It was certainly out of the question to look up again at the helicopter – but a receding volume of noise suggested this had already been directed to wait at a distance for further instructions. It would not be correct, to hover above the Queen's head – especially as Prince Harry, joined now by a new arrival at the picnic site, his brother William, could be seen emerging from the boathouse. The elder brother propelled his sibling in a wheelchair, and a slight girl, or young woman (she looked about twenty-seven years old) came from the boathouse to help push the chair up the steep incline to the picnicking area. Only the Prime Minister and his wife seemed curious to learn what exactly was taking place, in this tranquil spot where the sun, glorious in its release from the gloom and clouds of morning, gave a picture-postcard look to the scene. A bunch of minor royals, some discontented, others smiling, walked up and down on the grass. The Queen, apparently encouraged by the success of her efforts with the boar meat, now selected some random pieces of lamb, which gave a satisfying sizzle when placed over the burning charcoal. In her headscarf, light Fairisle knit and tartan skirt, she proclaimed the necessity of looking out for all kinds of weather in this part of the world. Her concentrated downward gaze on the assorted burning meats also demonstrated her intention to look out for nothing else.

The wheelchair proved intractable at the prospect of soggy terrain and steep gradient, and a decision was made to serve lunch on the platform of wood which acted as jetty and scenic sitting place at the boathouse. The black water of the loch lapped against the wide planks and was visible to those on the long benches constructed at the time of Victoria's reign as they sat and looked down at the submerged weeds and darting trout below. There was a sense of insecurity here, with the setting half aqueous and part solid, the oak stained by age to the colour of a seal's coat. And today, as Mrs MacDuff relieved Her Majesty of her barbecue implements and walked slowly down the bank after her, that sense of uncertainty appeared to have increased, despite the sovereign's calm and composure. No one dared mention the sudden appearance of the woman, blouse and skirt ripped by brambles, hair wild from falls against rock and in precipice. The chopper was by now no more than a faint hum in the distance. Nothing, so it might be possible to conclude, had come to disturb the dignity and appreciation of this fine day.

It was when the royal party was assembled, and the Queen finally seated in a large wooden chair garnished with stags' antlers and other mementoes of long-past shooting parties, that the unimaginable happened. People said afterwards that the Head Footman, John, in attendance by then with platters of the royal barbecue efforts and handing out the paper plates with which the royals liked to emulate the simplicity of a fête champêtre, should have seen the crazed nurse as she hurtled down the bank towards them, arms outstretched. Shouldn't John, usually so fleet of foot in dining-hall or nursery mealtimes, have leapt forward and somehow prevented the appallingly embarrassing scene? That he didn't might count against him (Mrs MacDuff thought this, and could not forgive herself for having been absent at that precise moment, cleaning the Gents Toilet in the boathouse and fussing in and out of the Ladies in order to escape the comments of Princess Michael). No, John would take the rap for this rare – if not unique – moment, when Her Majesty herself had no choice but to look up – and look.

'Wills!' The dim creature known as Sister Julia jumped from the path beside the jetty and ran up to the young Prince. Her eyes, without the unglamorous glasses she normally wore, shone; her hair, swept back in the breeze that made waves on the dark water, flew behind her, free from the bandeau she was never habitually seen without. And her voice – so different, Mrs MacDuff could swear when the odd scene drew her to the window and then out onto the jetty – so unlike her usual monotone, almost whispered way of talking, came loud and assured, if flat. 'Oh, am I glad to see you here!'

And she was greeted with smiles – again for just a moment, before the inappropriate nature of the occasion declared itself, and John finally stepped forward to escort the nurse from the family picnic she had chosen to interrupt so rudely.

The Queen must speak first, and, unusually, she was silent. Then conversation resumed, and, after a while, rain.

CHAPTER THIRTEEN

David Baron and Janet MacDuff were drinking a late cup of tea in Mrs MacDuff's sitting room. The picnic had just ended.

'It would seem,' said Mrs MacDuff, 'that Sister Julia has as many lives as a cat, as far as this establishment is concerned.' Her voice was harsh. She took a sip of her excellent tea. 'First the business of the ring – a case of theft, in my humble opinion but – no – the woman escapes all punishment. And then she takes off with Prince Harry without a word of warning and having somehow reassured the detectives – she must have lied about where she was going – and disappears with him for hours. To a drug clinic, of all places. Can you imagine what the press would have made of that, Mr Baron? It was a mercy you were following, and not them. Then she puts the whole place in uproar by abandoning that jeep. Full alert. Can you explain to me, Mr Baron, why that woman is not now in a taxi to the station? Or in the hands of the police, which she ought to be.'

'All I can suppose, Janet,' Baron said carefully, 'is that Her Majesty who, as we know has an eagle eye for a dangerous person, concluded she didn't want a fuss at the picnic because of a silly woman. And thinks the relationship between Prince Harry and his nurse is too valuable, at the moment, to destroy, for his sake.'

He spoke quite evenly. He picked up a piece of shortbread from the table and bit into it but there was something nagging at him, a thought he couldn't quite bring to the surface, a blurred image in his mind he couldn't quite see.

'In a deplorable state,' Mrs MacDuff was protesting. 'Unkempt

– buttons off her skirt. I've never seen anyone – anyone at all – present him or herself to Her Majesty in such a state. In my opinion the woman's a lunatic. You must tell the Prince's PS immediately, Mr Baron, about this trip to the drug rehab. They know she disappeared but I don't believe Sir James or anyone else knows where she went. That will make a considerable difference. Taking your patient out for some air and getting lost on the estate is one thing – haring round the public roads is another. Once that's known, she'll be gone for good.'

David Baron got a sudden flash of the boathouse and saw in his mind's eye Sister Julia's impulsive, lopsided rush towards Prince William. He wished he were not in Mrs MacDuff's parlour, a thin cup of Earl Grey in one hand and a piece of shortbread on a thin plate on the small table beside him. The room was too hot. He had been up since six that morning. Nevertheless, Baron's self-discipline was perfect. He sat, apparently at ease, showing no sign of impatience, his eyes attentively on his hostess.

'You'd be well advised to tell the Prince's Private Secretary about that trip to the drug clinic,' said Janet MacDuff. 'You're the only person who knows about it. Once Sir James hears, he'll act. The woman will be out in a flash.'

'Of course I'll tell him,' Baron assured her. But he needed time to think about that and so deflected Mrs MacDuff. 'I wonder who she really is?' he asked.

'That's what we'd all like to know,' Janet MacDuff said promptly. 'It's time they went through whatever credentials she offered with a toothcomb. There's been some slackness there.'

'You're an observant woman, Janet,' Baron said. 'And you've seen plenty of people moving through this palace. What's your instinct?'

'She hardly ever talks to anyone, except Prince Harry, and they're forever babbling together. But otherwise she just stands there with her eyes cast down, saying nothing. She was offered a place in the senior staff dining room but she said she'd be with her patient most of the time. She eats either with Prince Harry or in her room. And so she doesn't eat with other staff or talk to them. Some might call her shy but I wonder if she's not hiding something.'

'I don't like it,' said Baron. 'She may be dangerous.'

'She may be mad,' said Janet MacDuff. 'I earnestly suggest you inform Sir James about that trip to Fairbairn Lodge, forthwith.'

'Yes, indeed,' Baron said. And again saw Julia running, as far as her limp would allow, arms outstretched, towards the young heir to the throne. Then, saying he had to prepare for dinner, where he would be seated beside the widowed Countess of Clive, he thanked Mrs MacDuff and left. After he'd gone Janet MacDuff looked doubtfully at the door he'd closed so quietly behind him. Surely Mr Baron should go immediately to Sir James and tell him about Julia's unauthorised trip with Prince Harry? It was vitally important to get this mysterious figure away from Prince Harry and, indeed, the whole of the family. But something told her Mr Baron did not consider this a priority. Perhaps he knew best, she thought, and then stood up to go to the kitchens. It was time to make sure the new Irish crystal goblets had been unpacked – the Queen had asked specifically for them. There would be sixty for dinner that night, including, of course, the Queen and Prince Philip, Prince Harry making his first evening visit down-stairs, the Prime Minister and his wife and Prince William and the young unknown woman he had brought with him. Since the young woman, Alison Walker, might for all anyone knew, be a future Queen of England – though Mrs MacDuff doubted it – she had put her in the rooms where Edwardian salaciousness meant few visits from Her Majesty were probable. The boy she had placed near his mother. Mrs MacDuff trusted a visiting nanny would see it as a responsibility to keep an eye on the boy. She did not see making provision for an unat-tended child of seven as part of her duties. She went to the kitchen.

Having left Mrs MacDuff, Baron did not go straight back to the Lodge. Instead he took a corridor on an upper floor towards the study set aside for remote members of the Royal Family who might want to check their share prices, read a newspaper or send e-mails. He thought the room was unlikely to be in use. Once in the small, somewhat uncomfortable room, lined with books insufficiently interesting or important for the library, he settled behind the computer. The vision of Julia running was still with him. He found the password for the computer exactly where he would have expected to find it, taped to the bottom of the top right hand drawer of the desk, under a pile of stationery. He emailed Sebastian in London, guessing he would be in his office, getting ready to attend some PR or charity bash. Sebastian responded immediately, 'OK, sweetheart. But why, oh why, oh why? Have you got something for me?'

He sent back, 'Don't ask now. A mystery.'

Not long after, Baron was gazing at images on his screen, a woman marrying, leaving hospital with a baby, dancing, taking her children on a fairground ride, a woman alone, a woman in a series of glamorous dresses, a woman in a flak jacket and a helmet with a protective visor – a woman whose every move had been recorded, analysed, brooded over.

He was gazing at an image of the young bride in her wedding dress, riveted by the sight, appalled by what he was thinking. One idea was unthinkable, unless you believed in ghosts, another more plausible, but alarming. And then again, there might be nothing in it – perhaps he was losing his mind.

He jerked up in his chair as a door opened. 'Mr Baron,' said the footman in the doorway, 'I'm sorry. I thought the room would be empty. Lady Hogg's daughter wants to use the computer.'

'That's quite all right,' Baron said. 'I suddenly remembered I'd forgotten a birthday. I had to make amends quickly.' He smiled a rueful, charming smile, then bent to delete quickly what he'd been doing. 'Lady Hogg's daughter is free to use the room.'

'Thank you, sir,' said John. But before he left the room he quickly retrieved Baron's deleted e-mails. He stood still for a moment, considering, then assumed his accustomed footman's expression and left the room to go about his duties.

CHAPTER FOURTEEN

Julia took trouble over the rest of the day to keep herself to herself, whoever, as she overheard David Baron splutter into his mobile phone from her seat by Harry's bed back at the castle – Baron had just returned the Prince's box of DVDs – this self was actually thought to be. He'd been speaking to Mrs MacDuff. 'It's time we took steps, Janet. She's demented, I'd say. We can't risk keeping quiet about this any longer.' Baron, thinking himself alone on the expanse of landing outside the White and Gold Room, had babbled excitedly on. 'I mean, who does this woman think she is? OK, I'll call later – there's a favour I want to ask you when you've got a minute. Speak then.' And the equerry, attempting to shed his air of indignation and self-importance in preparation for entry into the invalid Prince's room, had sighed and raised his knuckles for the deferential tap at the door required of all royal servants. To find himself admitted by none other than Julia had clearly been a disconcerting experience – and for a while there was an impasse in the doorway, with neither Baron nor the nurse apparently able to move. Only Harry's laughter had freed them; and then, the box safely deposited in the corner by TV and old-fashioned record player, the equerry had bowed and withdrawn. But Julia had seen, from the last penetrating glance he directed at her, that she must lie low in future if she was to remain at Balmoral and care for her patient. There must be no more indulging in the strange mood of remembrance and melancholy which had overtaken her since she came north to this castle set in miles of heathered moor. She must live for today; and she knew it was as important for her to remember that she must ignore the possible fears of tomorrow just as it was dangerous for her to look back at the past.

'Julia, where on earth did you get to today?' Harry sat forward in bed and grinned. 'Grandma looked a bit – well, I thought she might flip when you crashed down the hill into the picnic. Not that she ever does – flip, I mean,' he went on after a moment's reflection. 'You didn't go up there – to the Lodge, I mean. Did you?'

Julia stayed silent, and for a time there was no sound in the room other than the faint whirring of a lawn mower outside and the distant movements of maids and footmen as they dusted and trudged, bearing trays and polishing ornaments and pictures. Harry thought of his father and of the woman who shared his life now, Julia knew – just as she did. They thought of the past, together: and this, as she had just determined, was strictly forbidden. 'Julia!' the boy called as she turned towards him, her eyes suddenly filled with tears: 'Julia, I'm so much better and Grandma said I could come down to dinner tonight. Will you come with me?'

Yes, the once-weak and pale young Prince did look considerably better, Julia acknowledged. Going round the bed to tidy Walkman, pens and coloured pencils (she had set him up like a child, Julia reflected, and he was one no longer) she rumpled his hair briefly and caught his look of appreciation. Of course he should go down to dinner with the grown-ups, she told him in a voice that was distant and authoritative – so much so that he now stared at her and frowned. The Prime Minister and his wife were of the party: it would be interesting to talk to them in the relative calm of a Balmoral evening. And the young Prince's brother – here Julia faltered once more, afraid to say the name and bring on another show of emotion. There had been no chance yet for the younger of the two royal boys to exchange jokes and banter with his brother, and dinner in the Great Hall at Balmoral would surely bring about the horseplay the siblings loved to indulge in.

'Yes, you should go,' Julia said as her charge gazed still in perplexity at her sad expression. 'But I can't – it wouldn't be right, you know.'

'But why?' Harry pleaded with her. 'I've asked MacDuff to tell John to lay a place for you – near me, in case I need help for something or other' – and here the boy's voice faltered, and Julia saw her patient was still in need of care and attention, after all. He'd had a hard time, suffering the accident, then pursued mercilessly out in Bali by world media… 'Of course. If the Queen doesn't mind,' Julia said slowly. It was hard to imagine a warm welcome from the boy's grandmother – or from the monarch's consort for that matter: there was no doubt the Duke of Edinburgh had witnessed the uncontrolled run down from the Burnwood to the picnic site earlier that day of the obscure nurse brought from the East to care for the young Prince. And the Duke was likely to be even less amused than the Queen at her letting herself go in front of royalty in that manner. Julia prayed for a seat somewhere along the vast table in the Great Hall where she would be unnoticed. Surely John would see to it that she went unseen, amongst the wives and unmarried daughters of lesser functionaries at the Court. 'So that's fixed then,' Harry said, a grin of relief brightening his face. 'Grandma won't mind, I promise you that.'

It was only ten minutes later, when she had left the White and Gold Room and crossed the first inner hall leading to the west wing, that Julia stopped short and found herself appalled at the idea of the evening ahead. What had Harry let her in for, she asked herself with mounting panic: how could she, so unused to any formal occasions in her quiet, regulated life as an aid worker, possibly cope with the etiquette, the stilted conversations required of a grand dinner party – the turning from one side to another at the correct moment during the meal? What, most worryingly of all, could she wear? The last thought, summoning visions of the black crossover dress or long embroidered skirt she had been accustomed to put on when a birthday or other celebration took place at the Relief Centre, transfixed her further to a place in the passage, just under halfway along the seemingly endless transit of the west wing. Why she had chosen this route she could not say; something in the crepuscular light, fed through glass arches high in the ceiling of the passage suggested an ancient memory, perhaps of a childhood game, had brought her here – and some seconds passed before the realisation came that it was not a memory of years past which held her here, but the real sound of a child's pain, coming from behind a door not ten feet away.

The sobbing was helpless – that was the word which came to Julia's mind as she went up the corridor and paused by a door of bright cedarwood, its reddish colour enhanced by the glass lights hanging at intervals along the passage. Cruel: she felt the word just as she saw the ugly redness of the door. Someone had been unforgivably cruel to a young child, and the victim could see no way of escaping misery and despair. Here, in this castle so often described as a 'fairy-tale' habitation for a Queen and her Princes and Princesses, a child knew degradation and dreadful sorrow. 'What is it?' Julia murmured as she turned the handle and went in. 'I'll help you – I'm here now. Tell me what's hurting and I'll see what I can do.'

The child sitting on the edge of a four-poster bed in the centre of an enormous room hung with rose-pink drapes and adorned with gold cherubs and ornately framed pictures on each available inch of wall, was a boy of about seven years old. A boy with long, untidy brown hair and a pale face. Eyes that were round and dark stared back at Julia, and the crying, slowly and reluctantly at first, ended. A square of tissue, soggy from over-use, was pulled from a pocket in a pair of jeans streaked with mud and dirt. 'I've lost my mother,' the boy said. And then, as Julia stood gazing down at him on the rich satin counterpane, 'I don't like it here. I want to go home.'

Julia dropped on her knees by the bed. She looked up at the boy, but his gaze was away from her, at the long window set high in the castle walls where only a strip of late afternoon sunlight and the long branch of a copper beech tree were visible signs of an outside world. He was like a wild child, she thought, refusing eye contact with a stranger, however friendly. He knew only one thing: that he was unhappy in this place, and lost in the labyrinth of passages, halls and spiral stairways that made up a baronial dream belonging to an age he knew nothing of. He was shocked, Julia saw – the immensity of the palace, the muted, mechanical movements of the servants as they went about their tasks and the sudden, alarming tokens of deference shown when a high-ranking person appeared, had thrown the child almost into a trance-like state. He would not respond to her affectionate gestures, her smile or her attempts to guess his name. Jack? Lou? Julia, still kneeling at the foot of the great ornamental bed, love couch of a long-forgotten Empress, threw out the names with abandon, hoping for the glimmer of a smile or recognition. But still the boy sat on.

'Will! Here he is! Jo-Jo, what have you been doing in here? My room's the seventh along the passage, you said you could count, mate. This is only number five!'

The boy slid from the rich satin quilt onto the floor and ran over to the young woman who, opening the door of the bed-chamber devoted to the art of Edwardian erotic pleasures, stood for a moment surprised by the décor, and its clear intent to titivate the senses. She had been at the boathouse, Julia realised: of course she had, and had spent most of the time indoors there, building a fire in the small grate of the mock sitting room in the hut built out over the loch: children loved to play house in this way, Julia knew, and she had liked the girl for giving herself wholeheartedly to the amusement of the little boy. It was only now, as she looked closer, that she realised the slight figure only spied from a distance, was in fact about twenty-seven or twenty-eight years old and clearly the mother of the child. And she was only halfway through appraising the features of the young woman who, grabbing little Jo by his collar in order to pull him back out onto the passage (thinking, perhaps, that this was the bedroom of the carer known as Sister Julia – she could have believed this, for her face showed a lack of worldliness unusual in these surroundings) – when footsteps, loud and boyish, sounded along the corridor and a tousled head came round the door, 'Alison! There you are!' said the young man who now appeared amongst them. 'I've been looking everywhere for you – and for Jo-Jo,' he added, giving a playful shove to the child which was returned with a mock salute and a wide grin. 'Are you coming out for a game of croquet, you two? I'll bet you've never played the game before – now have you, Joseph?'

Julia knew herself seen, noticed as all those near to royals must know themselves: the tremor of apprehension, the well-trained greeting, the moving on to the mouthing of further politenesses and the gradual reducing of the aura created by personality. But on this occasion, as she noted with pleasure and relief, there was a warmth and sincerity lacking in others born or wedded to the elevated state. William had grown up well: he was a tribute to a happy childhood and a rearing at the hands of one who had no time for hypocrisy and loved open-ness and truth. 'You must be Julia,' the new visitor to the great pink and white room now said, turning to her with a smile. 'I've heard a lot about you.' And, before Julia had time to reflect that, as with all royals, trained to ignore or forget embarrassing incidents, the Prince had chosen to erase from his mind the incident at the loch, the heir in direct succession to the British throne seized young Jo-Jo by the arm and marched him out again, heading off down the passage towards the centre of the castle and the Banqueting Hall. Julia was left to stare after him; and only Alison, as Julia now knew the Prince's girlfriend to be, was left by the door open into the chamber the child had mistaken for his mother's. There had been no time for her to acknowledge the identity of the Prince, Julia thought: he could have been a stranger to her, however well known his features and character might be to his grandmother's subjects: the future of the Crown depended on William, but she had given no sign of recognition to the boy! – she had been as lost as little Jo had been when she came in to comfort him earlier. But, 'Will hates it when people bow or curtsey to him, you know,' Alison said, as if she had guessed the nurse's discomfiture at showing a lack of respect to the Prince of Wales's son. 'He'd much rather just be ordinary – as far as possible, that is.'

Sensible, Julia reflected, and she smiled gratefully at this composed young woman, neither beautiful nor plain but in charge of her emotions and her independence, it was possible to see, in a way that could only benefit a young person beleaguered by false admiration and the manic attentions of the world press. Alison at William's side could make another big difference to the monarchy in coming years; and, silently, Julia prayed that neither prejudice nor extreme pressure would separate the two.

These thoughts, punctuated by the sound of an impromptu game of ping-pong – William had rushed to the long table in the Banqueting Hall, probably, and was knocking up with young Jo for the sheer fun of it – were definitely ended by the heavy footsteps and stentorian tones of the housekeeper Mrs MacDuff as she came along the corridor, keys in hand. For the first time since meeting the Prince's new friend, Julia realised fully what the poor girl was up against: if she can survive MacDuff, came the thought, then she can sit easy on the throne and ignore all the brickbats that come her way. 'Miss Walker?' the housekeeper said, her voice low and filled with a contempt she had not considered worth her while when addressing a possible thieving member of the temporary household staff. 'May I have a word with you, please? Your...' and here the voice deepened and furrows of disgust appeared between her eyes – 'your son has dirtied the eiderdown in his room. Now he has visited the Pompadour Room –' and the bunch of keys was waved in the direction of the still-open door. 'The lace counterpane on the four-poster there was crocheted by Her late Majesty Queen Mary. Betty will take it down to be cleaned and repaired.'

Julia felt like bursting out laughing – but a real fear of the housekeeper, she acknowledged to herself angrily, prevented her from doing so. Not so Alison Walker, Julia noticed with a concealed glee: the young woman laughed in disbelief, then asked politely if she could see the offending marks. 'I made him change out of his shoes, Mrs MacD, when we came back from the picnic. He made a big thing of it – but I'd brought the Nikes to make up for it. He knows he has to be careful here.'

'I didn't say the stains were mud,' Mrs MacDuff replied. Her tone was impassive, but the implication was clear. 'I am told a hyperactive child may lose control in this way.'

'What?' said Alison sharply.

But it was too late for retort or explanation. Reappearing at the end of the corridor and running together like children were William and Jo-Jo. 'We're practising for the Braemar Games,' William called out as he drew near and the housekeeper, back against the wall, sank into a deep obeisance. 'Jo's faster than I am – I'll have to tie him down to an egg-and-spoon race, at this rate.'

It was just as well, Julia thought a few moments later when on her way to the back stairs of Balmoral and the servants' quarters, that the mate William had found for himself had the intelligence and equanimity to overlook the housekeeper's appalling rudeness. Maybe, the nurse breathed to herself when the Banqueting Hall was crossed and the hard cord of the stairs behind the upper pantry was safely under her feet, maybe Alison will be able to survive the family, too. And with this cheering possibility in mind, she climbed the five floors to her small room. If she could instil a few more precepts into the handsome thoughtful boy who would one day be King – if he could understand more fully that the way of life of his grandparents and remaining parent was no longer acceptable to the people of the realm, then there was hope still for the country's most ancient institution. From what she had seen of her so far, Alison Walker was the one to set the Prince on the true course – with, as Julia acknowledged with a smile, a little help from herself along the way.

CHAPTER FIFTEEN

The door of Julia's room was open a few inches and evening sunlight poured through the aperture, making an orange fan on the cramped landing of the highest floor of the back stairs. With her hand on the doorknob, Julia paused: someone had been here; she knew the door had been carefully closed behind her earlier that day and she knew also that no one at the castle had any reason to go looking for Prince Harry's nurse high in the servants' quarters of Balmoral. This could only mean trouble – even after five years as a relief worker in a remote and unguarded area of Pakistan, where random ambushes and unforeseen killings and kidnaps were common currency, Julia recognised the fear she now experienced as greater than any apprehensions she had suffered there. She knew the shadow of invisible enemies, the need to protect and preserve a family, its standing and reputation in the country and across the globe – and the ability of those hidden antagonists to disguise themselves completely in the presence of their prey. Someone – one of these – had been here today, and had, quite blatantly, left the door ajar, a warning to the occupant of the humble room that flight or absence would prove more palatable than remaining in residence at the castle. Once the spreading tail of the sun had faded from the stairs and landing and the soft shades of gloaming descended over turrets and fortified walls, the room must be without sign of 'Sister Julia', the mysterious interloper in the lives of this great dynasty. This was a message and it was spelt in the crack of light between the doorjamb and plain, green-painted door: Leave now. There is still time. Go back to where you belong.

But Julia knew she belonged here. Standing still bemused by the blaze of evening sun on the landing, she tried to rid her mind of the preoccupations which had possessed her on the long walk from the wing where William's friend and her child had been housed, to the steep blackness of the back stairs. She had thought – wondered, rather – whether something good, even wonderful could come about, in the shape of the sovereign's approval of the unconventional match between a Royal Prince and future King and a young woman with none of the attributes expected of a Royal Prince's bride, a young woman who had either been married or lived with another, and borne his son. Could the Queen or her consort tolerate such a descent into the cesspit of ordinary life? – and if they could not, what would the response of the heir and his chosen partner be? Julia didn't know – this she had to acknowledge to herself. She didn't know whether revolt against an inherited position and all its privileges and curtailments stirred within the good-mannered, cheerful young man she had met briefly today. So much had happened since – but here Julia closed her thoughts and returned to the present and the fiery glow of the setting sun as it met the now fully open door to her room. She walked in, shading her eyes, and forgot all except what she saw there – and as she did so the glow subsided and the room resumed its normal proportions around her. Someone had been in here indeed; but nothing had been removed or destroyed. The opposite, it appeared, had taken place: an addition to Julia's wardrobe was clearly visible. She crossed the narrow room to the bed and stared down at the garment which lay, meticulously folded, on the austere coverlet provided by Mrs MacDuff for those who toiled as domestics for the Queen. Against this background, the tulle and sequins of a ball dress of twenty years before rested, ready to come forth and re-enact the scenes of an epoch long brushed away and dismissed by the housekeeper and her mistress.

Now Julia felt relief – at recognition of a kindly gesture (for a note signed 'John' pinned to the bodice, along with a gardenia from the royal greenhouse announced 'you may not have anything to wear at dinner tonight: you might like to try this') – and another kind of recognition, too, that of the impossibility of eradicating the past. This ghostly dress, the colour of the now soft blue light of the Scottish twilight which lay all around the castle and distant hills, was a tangible reminder of days when there had still been hope. The happiness of the young woman who danced in the diaphanous beauty of this dress was assumed by people everywhere. The bad days of disbelief and disillusion were still to come.

Julia closed the door of her room and sat on the hard upright chair by the small table under the window as evening gently superseded the blue hour and electricity made pinpricks of brightness in dark turrets and down in sculleries and kitchens already deep in gloom. It was time to put on that dress – if she was prepared to accept her patient's invitation and go down to dinner in the Banqueting Hall. She knew herself to be ready, she would go.

CHAPTER SIXTEEN

Wee Mary saw the ghost when she was in the pantry of the small sitting room at Balmoral. This was the room where the Queen entertained privately – and had been accustomed to sit with her mother while drop scones, Mrs Hepburn's speciality, were brought to the round table in the window overlooking the dahlia garden. Today the Prime Minister and his wife had enjoyed scones and honey and a slice of the walnut cake presented by Mrs MacDuff herself, always a marker of a special occasion. The Queen had been joined by the Duke of Edinburgh for afternoon tea – and this, wee Mary and her helper the under-housemaid Mary, had agreed was an extremely unusual occurrence as the Duke liked to spend this quiet stretch of the day with his carriage horses, or playing polo. Only the most pressing affairs of state brought Prince Philip to his wife's side in the small sitting room for tea.

It would have been impossible for wee Mary to say what it was that the Prime Minister was determined to discuss with his sovereign and her consort, but it was remarked afterwards that only the Prime Minister's wife had enjoyed the drop scones, brown and yellow on the underside and soft as a dachshund's ears. These came piping hot up from the kitchen in the antiquated little pantry lift installed by the late King Edward VII to facilitate the entertaining of ladies – and also to ensure the easy availability, should he require them, of chicken drumsticks in breadcrumbs, a prophylactic against the hunger pangs caused by anxiety. Today, despite a high level of tension, exhibited not only by the presence of Prince Philip but also by the white knuckles showing on the monarch's crooked finger as she held her teacup, there had

85

been few takers for the cucumber sandwiches, lemon-icing-covered sponge fingers – or even the housekeeper's solid walnut cake. Nerves caused starvation, not stuffing, as in the days of the Queen's grandfather. Something monumental was under discussion. And to reach for a thrillingly slender pastry disc, something between a macaroon and a plain biscuit and known at the castle as a Melting Moment, would have removed the gravity of the moment indeed. History was in the baking, here; and only Mrs B, as she was known semi-affectionately in royal circles, ignored the weightiness of the occasion and munched on.

For all the import of the conversation – and even Mary, who had become accustomed to closing her ears to royal exchanges since being caught at the Lodge gates on the southern drive to Balmoral by a tabloid newspaperman demanding to know whether Princess Margaret had gone to Ballater, the nearest town, and purchased her own cigarettes there (naively, Mary had replied that Her Royal Highness had gone to make a telephone call from a call box to her married boyfriend: the succeeding splash on the front pages had had Mrs MacDuff lining up the chambermaids and docking wages) – for all the epoch-making content of the royal and ministerial talk, Betty was not able to say later that the heir to the throne of Britain and his paramour were now definitely engaged to be married. There was mention of the Archbishop of Canterbury, certainly; but at this point Mary dropped the tongs, essential equipment for dealing with the chocolate sticky cake and engraved with the initials of the late Queen Elizabeth, the Queen Mother, a gift from her birthplace, the haunted castle of Glamis. A puddle of dark chocolate spread across the surface of the rosewood table. Betty had to run in from the pantry with a cloth. She was shaking all over, as she whispered to Mary once they were back in the damp little room dominated by a huge enamel sink and the famous lift which rattled up and down with crockery and spoons. She had looked out of the window above the sink and seen the ghost there, walking on the higher level of the garden above the dahlias. And the ghost was – no doubt about it, she'd swear on it any day of the week – the image of Princess Di.

Then the little bell rang in the small sitting room. The Queen wanted the tea things cleared: the Prime Minister and his wife were already standing, and Prince Philip's slight inclination of the head indicated that he looked forward to meeting his guests later at dinner. There was talk in low voices, a sense of impending announcements, a movement of feet on deep pile carpet. The maids, heads down and bustling, pulled back the royal chair and waited, backs against the wall, for the sovereign's departure. 'Such a delicious tea,' the Prime Minister's wife breathed as she looked into the pantry – but, to her slight concern, neither of the maids turned to accept her compliments. Their eyes were fixed on the window above the sink. For – and both were to agree on this while clearing the barely-eaten feast from the table in the small sitting room – the ghost remained visible for several minutes after Betty's first sighting. It only became impossible to see, in fact, when it moved out of frame and walked down the wide flight of stone steps into the lower garden in order to enter the house. The prospect of finding The Blue Lady, as Betty and Mary named her – for neither had the courage to refer to the ghost by the name it had borne when alive – brought enjoyable shivers and shudders right up to the time when they would be required to assist with the preparation of the table for dinner. Even the ghost of the Princess, it appeared, was of greater interest to the girls than the probable forthcoming nuptials of the heir to the throne.

The evening air was balmy as the Queen and her Prime Minister stood on the balcony outside the small sitting room, talking quietly. The sun was going down on the green and blue hills opposite them.

In her half century reign the Queen had had dealings with ten Prime Ministers, since Harold Macmillan, who had been to her rather as the powerful, avuncular figure of Lord Palmerston had been to Queen Victoria. Of late she believed she had noticed in some of her Prime Ministers a concealed resentment of her position. Each wanted the country to have a President, and each wanted the President to be him or her. As mere Prime Ministers they had their status only because the MPs of their own party had voted them in. They felt at a disadvantage when faced in international negotiations, with men and women elected by the whole population. This Prime Minister, though, did not seem to be a man with presidential ambitions, so far. He did not give Her Majesty the idea that he wanted her job. 'I wonder, Prime Minister,' she said, 'if you would give me the benefit of your advice.'

'Of course, ma'am,' he replied. 'If I can help in any way.'

The Queen got to the point rapidly. 'You will know,' she said, 'that the Archbishop of Canterbury is sounding the bishops about the remarriage of divorced people.'

'Yes, Ma'am, I do know. I gather so far half are prepared to consider this, the other half not. Of course, the results aren't complete.'

'I don't think when they are they'll be very much different,' said the Queen. 'So there'll be no clear answer from the bishops. The Archbishop could then choose to put the matter to the Anglican Synod, but he might hesitate to do so. It's a topic likely to cause a division between the more conservative Anglicans and the others. The Archbishop would prefer to avoid a schism.'

'I see,' said the Prime Minister. He was not sure where this conversation was leading. It was probably connected with the marriage of Prince Charles. But even if the Church of England agreed to marry divorced people Prince Charles would still be unable to marry Mrs Parker Bowles as she was already married to a Roman Catholic. Under the Act of Settlement of 1701 any member of the Royal Family who chose to marry a Catholic – or a person of any other faith at all – would have to renounce any claim to the throne. The Prime Minister knew, like any sane person, that this Act was out of date, but it existed and if it were to be changed, it would have to be changed in Parliament.

The truth, of course, was worse. 'You understand that His Royal Highness, Prince Charles,' she said clearly, 'has it in mind to announce his engagement to Mrs Parker Bowles. He believes that if he does so the public and the Anglican Church will back him.'

This prospect horrified the Prime Minister. The future King was about to attempt to bounce the public and the Anglican Church into agreeing to his marriage. This was of course what his predecessor, Henry VIII, had done, but Henry had behind him the rope, the axe and the right to burn his opponents at the stake. All the Prince had was public opinion and the Prime Minister had not the same confidence as Prince Charles that public opinion was on his side.

The Prime Minister did not want to mention the two D words. He knew much of the public was still against the royal marriage on various grounds, depending on age and sex. Some disliked Mrs Parker Bowles's perceived role in the break-up of the Prince's earlier marriage to Princess Diana. Some rejected the idea of a marriage because they didn't fancy Mrs Parker Bowles themselves. Others thought the couple too old and too plain to be in love at all, let alone to get married. The second D was even more sinister from the Prime Minister's point of view. If the Anglican Church could not agree to marrying the Prince and Mrs Parker Bowles the spectre of Disestablishment, the separation of Church and State surfaced. He knew the Church of England didn't want this, and suspected the Queen felt the same. For his own part, he dreaded the unravelling which would take place, enough to keep constitutional lawyers in work up to the next election, and beyond.

His monarch had sought his advice and, at risk of possibly chilling the relationship during the course of his premiership, he would give it. He was not a son of the manse for nothing.

'I can only say, ma'am, that it's my opinion His Royal Highness should reconsider. The public might not like it, the Church might not like it. There's no certainty. There are no guarantees. Assuming the Church of England agreed to marry the divorced, we might remove the Act of Settlement, which would allow Mrs Parker Bowles, as a Catholic, to marry the Prince. Some might argue the change is overdue, but it could be seen as a move purely to facilitate His Highness's marriage. The public could react badly. Again, it's impossible to say. The marriage otherwise would involve Mrs Parker Bowles changing her faith. This would obviously be her decision, but it might be useful to consider the fact that there are large and vigorous Catholic communities in almost all Commonwealth countries and they might not take kindly to Mrs Parker Bowles's choice to join the Anglican community.'

He suspected that his last point might be the only consideration the Queen had not thought about long and hard. Her Majesty was very attached to the idea of the Commonwealth.

'It is a complicated affair constitutionally,' he said. 'Perhaps you will give me your permission to speak to His Royal Highness, to urge delay.' It was not a duty he welcomed, but it was a duty he knew he had to undertake.

'Of course. I hope you can persuade him,' she said.

'I'll do my best,' he told her. But he imagined the Queen had already made to the Prince of Wales all the points he had made to her. And so, he guessed, had his father, in no uncertain terms. What might dissuade the Prince would be if he, like caliphs of old, assumed a disguise and went into the bazaars – or the pubs – to find out what people really thought of him and his affairs. This was unlikely.

'Perhaps we should think about getting ready for dinner,' said the Queen.

The Queen and her Prime Minister parted outside the sitting room in silence. What they both knew but could not say was that apart from the constitutional questions it might raise, which most people didn't understand and didn't want to (and who wanted a multi-faith nation to understand the issues too clearly?), the whole affair was shadowed by a figure from the past, the never-to-be-forgotten Princess Diana. She had started off as a pawn in the royal game and ended up as a queen, whether a black or white queen depended on how you looked at it.

CHAPTER SEVENTEEN

Colin lay on his bed in darkness. It was dark outside the windows although Colin knew that the view in daylight was of farmland and stone-strewn fields in which cattle grazed. He felt numb, although a corner of his mind nagged and jumped, that corner that wanted, needed, a fix. It was nearly midnight now and it had been a long day – a very long day. Across the room the man he shared with was asleep, sleeping the sleep of the just – or was it? Colin himself was finding it hard to sleep. What was he doing here? The question he had been asking himself, intermittently all day. He was getting clean, thanks to Julia. 'Don't come back,' she'd said. Well, it looked as if, now, the opportunity to do that wouldn't be there. So where would he go?

After his arrival at the rehab clinic that morning Colin had been led into a wide entrance hall. There were paintings on the wall and elaborate flower arrangements on half-moon tables on either side. Through an open door to the left was a large reception room, the door on the right showed a dining room, with small tables. Dr Cassidy, a small plump man with a heavy black moustache, had introduced himself outside and now led him through the hall, down a small corridor to his consulting room.

Dr Cassidy sat down behind his desk, Colin sat obediently in front of him and the doctor took him through his basic history – family background, health, education, employment and history of addiction. Colin stumbled through the answers, feeling more and more uneasy. He had had his last fix the night before. The morning had started tough and was growing tougher by the minute. He didn't dare ask the doctor for something to help. At the end of the interview, though, Dr Cassidy put down his pen and said, 'There – not too painful, was it? Now, here we don't advocate the use of methadone. That's often the way of substituting one drug for another. We'll be going into the whys and wherefores of addiction in our counselling sessions, which are daily, one-on-one with your physician and group sessions.'

Colin's heart sank. If it was going to be cold turkey, he was out of here, Julia or no Julia. But the doctor was still speaking: 'What we give you is a cocktail of my own devising, to ease the problem of withdrawal. We reduce the amounts as your dependency declines.' He stood up, produced a key ring and unlocked the door of a connecting room. He went in and came out shortly after with a plastic cup full of colourless liquid. He handed it to Colin. 'Down the hatch,' he remarked encouragingly. He picked up the phone, 'Can you tell Edward Manningham to wait for me in the hall. I have his new roommate with me.' To Colin he said, 'Edward will show you your room and tell you all about what happens here. There's a booklet for you in your room – rules and regulations.'

But no Edward Manningham arrived in the hall. Dr Cassidy caught a short fair young man who was crossing the hall with a couple of squash rackets in his hand and asked, 'David – can you take Colin here up to his room?'

'Pleased to,' said David willingly. He bounded up two flights, Colin puffing behind and opened the door to a large well-furnished room, where flowers stood on a table under a window. At either side to the room was a single bed, covered by a white coverlet. Colin's companion flung open a door. 'Bathroom,' he announced. Colin was impressed. The place was like a hotel.

'It's nice here,' he ventured. He was beginning to feel woozy as the cocktail took effect.

'There's a booklet on the table saying what's expected of you. You're meant to read it straight off. You have to take responsibility for yourself,' he assured Colin. He looked him in the eye and asked, 'Have you acknowledged Christ as your personal saviour?'

Colin hardly knew what to say. Honesty, he decided, was the best policy. 'No, I haven't,' he admitted.

'Do so,' advised the fair young man. 'It helps – it transforms you.

We'll have a talk later. Just now, I have to go. I have a date to play squash. The gym's in the basement.' He went to the door. 'Lunch is at one. Don't forget about our chat.'

'Right,' said Colin. After David had gone he went and lay down on what he assumed would be his own bed. He'd been without a fix before, often enough, so he knew what Dr Cassidy had given him was quieting the scream in his head and the rat gnawing in his guts. It helped, but it was not enough. Still, he owed it to Julia to give it a go, he thought. Though that wouldn't be easy if the place was full of born-again Christians, which was what David seemed to be. It could be hard, too, if the patients were all as smart as the premises. He was an estate-worker's boy. If the place was full of posh loons, the kind who carried the guns while he acted as a beater, then he might not be able to bear it.

He dozed. He had no watch. He had once had one, a Christmas present, but that had gone with most of his own property, and some of other people's, in exchange for drugs. He was half-asleep when a voice from the door said, 'Oh – hey – sleeping beauty – you have to get up. Lunch. You don't get to miss any meals here. It's the rules. They sent me up to get you.'

Colin swung his feet to the floor. 'Thanks,' he said. He looked over at a tall, attenuated figure. The other man had close-cropped brown hair and a long pale face. He wore black jeans and an Arran sweater. Posh loon? Not posh loon? Colin couldn't decide. 'Colin?' enquired the tall man. 'No offence, man, but you'd better get a shower and a shave before you come down to lunch. They're fussy like that.'

'The rules,' Colin said wearily.

'Better than a Thai jail,' said the other.

'You'd know?' asked Colin.

'The good news – they've left you some spare clothes,' his companion pointed out. On a chair near the door lay a pile of clothes, corduroy trousers and a sweater. 'The bad news – the previous owner topped himself.'

'Are you serious?' asked Colin.

The other man looked at the pile more closely. 'The trousers look quite familiar. I'm your roomie, Edward Manningham.'

Colin advanced. They shook hands briefly. Edward's hand was cold, eye contact brief. Colin was dazed and Edward's eyes had the thousand-yard stare of a battle-worn Vietnam veteran. Colin picked up the clothes from the chair and went into the bathroom. He was out in less than ten minutes, showered and shaved and wearing the fresh clothes and his old, battered trainers. Edward was still waiting and they went silently downstairs together. They sat down at a table for four in the dining room. The other two were a young woman with a long brown plait and a man of about fifty wearing a V-necked blue lambswool sweater, a well-starched shirt and a tie striped with the colours of a club, school or regiment. The veins in his face were broken. He looked very depressed as he spooned up apple pie and custard. The young woman was eating a pear. Names were exchanged and after that no one spoke. There was very little sound from the other tables, where some twenty others sat. It reminded Colin of the kind of tea room he used to go to with his parents on holiday, only there was less conversation.

A maid came up with two plates covered by metal covers. Underneath were two lamb chops and some vegetables. Colin felt sick. He looked at his plate.

'The vegetables are all home-grown,' the young woman, Corinna, said encouragingly.

'We grow them,' Edward said without enthusiasm. He ate a piece of one of the chops. Others were beginning to leave the dining room. One girl was weeping as she left, with the arm of another over her shoulders. The waitress came back and tutted as she picked up Colin's plate. 'Fruit or pudding?' she asked.

'Fruit,' Edward answered for both of them. Corinna got up to go. 'What's on this afternoon, Corinna?' Edward asked.

'Don't you ever look at your programme?' Corinna enquired. 'Garden and one-to-one for Blues, group therapy for Greens.'

A woman in a white coat came and collected Colin for a full medical. She gave him a couple of pills and sent him off. The whole house, when he left the medical room seemed very silent and empty. He went up the echoing staircase. On the table, now, was a schedule of activities for the next seven days, with his name at the top – therapy with Dr Cassidy, group therapy, gardening, exercise. His dirty clothes had been taken from the bathroom. He slept again.

Supper was formal. The tables were covered with cloths, three courses and even a glass of wine, red or white, was on offer. Dr Cassidy and others of the staff sat at one table.

Colin sat, again, with Corinna and the older man. He began to discuss his medication, but no one responded. He told Colin, 'I used to run the biggest hotel in Sutherland.'

'Is that so?' said Colin.

'Did you get any whisky from Manningham and Massie?' Edward asked, plainly not caring about the answer.

'I don't believe we did,' the man answered. 'Is Manningham your father?'

'Manningham and Massie, whisky distributors to five counties,' recited Edward. 'Fancy a game of snooker after supper?' he asked Colin.

'Why not?' Colin replied.

The games room was dimly lit and deserted, except for two young men sitting on the floor under the dart board. Colin thought they looked stoned.

While Edward picked the scattered pages of a tabloid newspaper off the snooker table Colin retrieved the balls from the pockets and put them on the table. Straightening up with some of them in his hand he saw that Edward was bent over the table, peering down at part of the paper. 'Well, I'm buggered,' he said. 'I know this guy.'

Colin started sorting out the snooker balls. 'What guy?' he asked.

'This guy in the paper. Used to be married to Prince William's new girlfriend. News to me – he never said anything about a wife. But I know it's him. Charlie Crawford, the Casanova of Bangkok. He's called Sutcliffe here, but he always had a bunch of passports –' He bent over the paper and looked more closely, 'Yeah, that's Charlie Crawford, right enough.'

'Why did they call him Casanova?' asked Colin. He wished Edward would stop looking at the paper and begin to play. Suddenly, he really felt like snooker. He was starting to feel bored and confined. He wanted to do something, anything to relieve the monotony.

'His gig was – he'd find a girl, a secretary on her holidays or a girl on her gap year, somebody clean, maybe British, Canadian, American, Australian and really sweep her off her feet. But only if he had enough money to get back to Britain, Canada, wherever and start a little business. And all it would take is the woman to take one little package to some address in London, Melbourne – just one. Then she'd get paid, he'd get paid and in no time at all he'd be there, putting down a payment on a house, starting the business – wedding bells, a little nest, all that. Of course, once the package was in safe hands Charlie stayed exactly where he was. There were a lot of tear-stained letters and phone calls – sometimes he'd have to go into hiding when a girl turned up looking. But it worked like a charm. He'd do it fifteen, sixteen times a year – he'd have two women on the go at once – but hardly any of them got caught.

'All you had to do, he said, was let them do the work. They'd invent what they wanted you to be and what they wanted you to say. You just had to go along.' He looked down at the paper again, 'Yes, that's Charlie. Nice looking woman, his wife, and a kid – he's younger here – this'll all be before he went to Thailand.'

Colin went to stand beside him. He looked down at the newspaper. The story covered two pages. 'Is this William's new love?' a headline read, over a picture of Prince William and a woman in a loose top and trousers, coming out of a cinema hand in hand. They were both smiling. 'Sutton single parent has dates with William' read another headline. '"A very nice young man," says building society manager, John Walker (52).' There was another picture of a middle-aged couple, the young woman said to be Prince William's girlfriend and a little boy, picnicking on a beach. There was a sandcastle and a bucket and spade in the corner of the picture. The photograph Edward was staring at showed a young couple, the girl in a simple white dress with flowers in her hair, the young man in a suit, with a buttonhole.

'Somebody's sold the family snaps,' Edward said. He read out, '"William is due to join the Queen for the annual Balmoral holiday. Will single parent Alison go with him to meet the Queen?"'

'I don't envy her if she does,' Colin remarked. 'They'll give her hell.'

'Yes?'

'They won't even know they're doing it, half of them. But wait until she meets the housekeeper – she's a rottweiler.'

'How do you know?'

'My Dad works on the estate.'

Edward stared at him. 'The royals pay for you to come here?'

Colin snorted. 'No way. They'd throw me out if they knew. Throw my Dad and Mum out, too. Well, that's what my Dad and Mum think, anyway. That's what they're afraid of.' He didn't want to discuss Julia's part in his being at the clinic. He asked, 'You're sure this is this Charlie?'

'If not, it's his identical twin. Tell you what – there's his right hand in the picture. Charlie'd lost the top of his right little finger. Can you see if it's there?'

'Not in this light,' Colin said. 'It might need a magnifying glass.' He looked at Edward, who stared straight back. 'Are you thinking what I'm thinking?' he asked.

'Yes, Colin. I do believe I am,' said Edward. 'What we need now is a magnifying glass.'

'And a phone,' Colin said.

CHAPTER EIGHTEEN

The table in the Great Banqueting Hall, laden with crystal and china, adorned with ornamental candelabra in gold filigree and resplendent with polished silver reflected in pools of light on the ancient oak of its surface, was like an archaic and beautiful animal, Julia thought, a great creature from under the sea, the fossil of a whale, beached in the luxury of a bygone age. Flowers – peonies and dark, scented roses, tall lilies and foliage from the trees in Balmoral's Prince Albert park, formed a succession of centrepieces on a medieval board at least forty metres long; and, like acolytes of the regal vases small clusters of violets and cyclamen nested in miniature glass bowls, exuding a woody aroma. The tapestries on the walls of the chamber, lit by pale tapers in sconces, echoed the theme of war, conquest and kingly pride spelt out at the great feast. Spears rose high in knotted wool and silk, against pointed Flemish hats and white-faced huntsmen, riding behind their sovereign. It was as if, and here she felt herself an outsider, an observer who would soon find herself no longer permitted to observe the reckless expenditure of the Royal Household, its determination to demonstrate power and influence through the flaunting of wealth and priceless possessions, there need never be any change or progress in this world where, so it was believed, all important decisions had long ago been taken from the Queen. If so, Julia reflected, why the sense of awe as Her Majesty, bound in ropes of pearls and diamonds, precious down to her dress stitched with jewels and the sparkling tiara in her white hair, came at last into the Great Hall and paused by her chair? All but Prince Harry, at Julia's side and seated in his wheelchair, were standing as the monarch glanced carefully at the assembled guests. Beside the Prime Minister and his wife were three other former Prime Ministers, two dukes and several members of the Beauclerk family, owners of the vast adjacent estates. Minor royalty, dotted around the table, looked like photographs of themselves, cut out and pasted onto cards – so Julia thought, recognising the contemptuous droop of a high-born lip here, or the receding forehead of a woman to whom these banquets, suffered for duty's sake, could only be got through when dreaming of a gallop in pursuit of a fox across Gloucestershire fields and woods. The Queen had not been able to prevent the ending of a royal sport emblazoned in the hanging pictures and tapestries on the walls. She could refuse to permit the declaration of war – so it was said, at least – but her subjects, as with so many other vaguenesses in the Constitution, were not sure about this. Yet – and as the consort of her long reign joined her at table, Julia looked down suddenly, aware she had been noticed by him – the atmosphere of power here tonight at Balmoral was almost palpable. It was heightened, too, by the sense of a special occasion: Julia couldn't help wondering, with a painful consciousness of coming regret, remorse, even unhappiness, whether an announcement of the engagement was due tonight. For, just as Prince Philip, seated a micro-second after his wife and polishing his gold-rimmed glasses the better to consider the woman placed by his younger grandson, stared down through a thicket of blooms and an army of gold candlesticks at the obscure nurse, so the eyes of every-one else were fixed on a couple seated high in the Queen's section of the board. Charles and Camilla: they glowed and beamed, seated together as if at a formal banquet in the City of London: recognised by the Head of State, secure and about to receive the felicitations of the assembled crowd. When the announcement came, after the *bisque* and the River Dee salmon and the saddle of lamb and the towering confections of meringue and Scottish raspberry with tossed cream, history would have moved to accommodate the heir to the throne. Toasts would be drunk and speeches made. The resident piper would circle the immense table, his tartan pleats swinging below a neat black velvet jacket. In this most invented and improbable castle, a forth-coming marriage as unreal as the turrets and gargoyles and dreamt-up tartans of Balmoral, would be declared. And the courtiers and dukes and ministers would raise their glasses to it, as they did for all the other rustled-up traditions of the country when there was a need.

But Harry – now the table was seated and the Queen had turned to her right, to the Prime Minister and the Duke of Edinburgh, keeping his pince-nez firmly in place, gazed still over the head of the Prime Minister's wife down a great swathe of table to Julia – Harry was talking and it was time for her thoughts to cease. 'Julia –' the young Prince, dwarfed in his low electric chair by the sheer largeness of the other men at table, looked small and pale. Blotches of colour had appeared on his cheeks. 'Why did they put Alison right down there, d'you think? I mean, she doesn't know anyone here – she must be *lonely*. Let's try and swap her seat with – well, the Gloucester woman, shall we?'

It was true, Julia realised with a pang. She had been busy thinking of the impossible grandeur of the boys' family – and of herself, she had to admit, and her coming reaction to the possible announcement – and had failed to see William's girlfriend at all. William, of course, was high up the table, near the Queen. Alison, placed between Prince Charles's equerry and Sir Rory Campbell, the newly appointed Governor of The Cheque, was as far from the one friend she possessed in the castle, as could be. I should have waved, Julia thought, and promptly did so the next time Alison looked around. The girl's face lit up and they exchanged smiles. In a simple dress and without any jewellery, the possible future Queen of England looked an unlikely guest at the feast. But they'll change all that if they get their hands on her, Julia said to herself, and sighed.

'And I was going to say, why couldn't Jo-Jo come down to dinner?' Harry went on as Julia, feeling herself trapped by the gaze of Charles's equerry, this rivalling in intensity that of the distant Duke of Edinburgh and a great deal more hostile, tried to concentrate on the young Prince's demands. 'I don't think your grandmother would like it,' she began, aware of sounding feeble. 'I did see Jo just before it was time for dinner and I told him to come down here if he was unhappy,' she added. 'But I asked Grandma and she said, "I'll see,"' protested Harry. 'She must have forgotten. Just think what an uncool time Jo is having, eating supper in the old nursery with MacDuff!'

David Baron, unlike the far-off Prince Philip, had no need for eyeglasses when it came to staring at Julia. She saw him ingest her – there was no other word for it – and again the image of a fish, this time a smooth fish by the great gold-ornamented hulk that was the banqueting table came to her. He would eat her alive, this cunning, deferential courtier, if she wasn't careful. He already mistrusted and hated her, she knew. Who would want to rid the castle of the troublesome Julia more than Baron, when the announcement came? He had seen the possible implications of her uncontrolled run down from the Burnwood and the White Lodge: he sensed the ambiguity of the woman who appeared sometimes to conduct herself like a tourist in her own past. No, this kind of trespassing on royal harmony could not occur again.

A figure appeared in the doorway to the Great Hall. It was small and it wore jeans and a pyjama top – as if a struggle had recently taken place over when and whether to succumb to pressure and go to bed. 'I don't like it up there,' Jo-Jo said, his quiet words audible in the sudden silence. 'Julia said I could come down if I wanted. Where's my Mum? I want to go home.'

CHAPTER NINETEEN

It could have been any family, sprawled on bean bags and feet up on the sofa, hair messed up after a long evening succeeded by games and mock wrestling matches, eyes bleary from laughing, which occupied the White and Gold Room that night. The tall, narrow hospital bed, it was true, showed that accommodation had been made for the victim of an accident – and the careful arrangement of TV, sound system and video and DVD player demonstrated an unusual amount of care and expense had been lavished on the patient, who sat now, restored to invalid status, against high, goose-feather pillows. Otherwise, an absence of restraint and a strong sense of delight in freedom, were noticeable in the room. Unself-conscious – this was the word which came to Julia, as she drew young Jo into the circle, passing him packs of cards for a reshuffle before a second round of Racing Demon. This was life as it was meant to be lived, with grown-ups and children all together when and where they wanted; and how far this picture of amicable jollity was from the occasions organised by the Royal Family needed no emphasising. It was as if, Julia thought contentedly as Harry and William and Alison and Jo drew round the rug for a game, everyone breathed for once without looking over a shoulder for spies, courtiers or photographers. Something in the clear affection between the elder of the two Princes and the straightforward, clear-eyed young woman invited to a palace for the first time – and incapable, as Julia saw, of manifesting either awe or deference – helped to make this liberated atmosphere possible. And Harry's pleasure at his brother's happiness blew away any possibility of awkwardness. This was the most delightful moment, Julia reflected, that she had experienced for years. A dream, a miracle: and to know herself welcomed as part of the close family group was both poignant and highly flattering. If only it could go on forever – but, as she recognised silently, even as they played, their anonymity (for who could have said, if shown a picture of them now, that these were Princes of the royal blood? William, with an ancient nightcap snaffled from the wardrobe pulled down over hair and eyes; Harry shielding his face with a hand of cards, features set in a mask of mock-pomposity, could have been anyone's boys, not heirs to the crown of the British Isles) was likely to be ended before morning. Mrs MacDuff, infuriated by Jo's escape from supper under her jurisdiction in the old nursery, would have gone looking for Julia by now; and, failing to find her in her room on the back stairs, would be waiting her time to catch the nurse when she left Prince Harry's room. The Prince of Wales's equerry, David Baron – Julia shivered and promised to herself that she would enjoy this rare interlude without thinking of Baron. For she knew in her heart that if anyone would end her time here with the beloved boys, it was the respected equerry of Prince Charles.

'Let's play forfeits.' Harry's voice rang out, and despite her pledge to herself, Julia looked anxiously at the door – as if trying to seek reassurance that the fact he was still up and about would not now be known all over the castle. She thought of the landings and corridors, the inner halls and rows of thick-walled rooms which separated the White and Gold Room from the austere quarters allotted to male attendants and courtiers to the Queen and her son. What nonsense! – of course Harry went unheard. And hadn't both the boys shouted earlier in their imitation fights, Harry seizing as a weapon a bolster from the bed. 'Very well,' Julia agreed. 'Forfeits – or Postman's Knock – whichever you think best, dear.' As soon as she spoke, she regretted her words: Postman's Knock, as the name implied, necessitated the player leaving the room and knocking on the door before entering to bestow a kiss on the holder of a number called out by another. Refusal to comply resulted in the forfeit of an article of clothing. And Julia had a strong suspicion, now, that someone did indeed stand outside the door of the White and Gold Room, and that it was not a member of Security. 'I'll go out first,' Alison offered, demonstrating not for the first time an understanding of Julia's concerns.

The game went without interference – and Julia considered herself fortunate, as William removed his white tie, already loosened and now handed over amid gales of laughter, to the 'postman' Alison in return for a hearty kiss, that the innocent little party had not been discovered and ordered to stop the fun. Perhaps, just for once, there could be a lack of protocol, a sense that the Lord of Misrule, a hero of Harry's in the days when he read fairy tales, had visited the castle tonight and they could let themselves go.

'Number twenty-one.' This was Julia's number, and it was spoken from behind the closed door. 'Come on, Julia, own up!' Harry cried. 'Twenty-one kisses for you,' and he waved to young Jo to join in a raid on the nurse. 'OK, we'll have your jacket then!' as Julia, flushed and laughing, wriggled away from the shower of kisses directed by all three boys. 'Come on, Julia, off with it!'

A knock at the door interrupted the scene. It wasn't Alison's knock – although it was she who first stepped into the room, as if shoved from behind by the new visitor. Laughter and talk died down as soon as David Baron appeared: it was as if, Julia thought in a flash of panic, the courtier had been sent by a Tudor monarch to announce the imminent execution of a wrongdoer in their midst. She flinched, and looked pointedly away from the equerry.

But Baron did not look away from the woman he had been informed was known only as Sister Julia to the Prince of Wales's household. He did not, however, attempt to look the nurse in the eye.

For he saw – as Julia was caught removing the light silk bolero jacket over her evening dress and her shoulders and neck were exposed – that an object dangled on a thin gold chain, there. Baron had not been in the employ of the Prince of Wales at the time of the celebration of his marriage with Lady Diana Spencer, but he had heard stories about the ring – a signet ring engraved with the Prince of Wales's feathers – sent round to Clarence House and presented to the bride-to-be on the eve of the wedding. How a messenger had almost picked up and delivered a pair of cufflinks, just received by the groom from his mistress, by mistake, and how he'd nearly lost his job for it. Baron remembered all this as he stood just inside the door of the White and Gold Room, staring at Sister Julia, who now struggled back into the jacket, thus concealing the pendant on its chain. She must have kept it ever since

– he remembered later that the thought had crossed his mind. What he said at the time was, 'His Royal Highness the Prince of Wales has asked if His Royal Highness Prince William of Wales and His Royal Highness Prince Harry of Wales are to be found here as Her Majesty the Queen wishes to say goodnight, as does his Royal Highness Prince Charles'.

The boys, the elder pushing the younger in his wheelchair, were followed out of the room by the equerry. They looked round and gave rueful shrugs before disappearing down the expanse of the landing. Julia and Alison and Jo whispered goodnight before going off to their distant rooms.

CHAPTER TWENTY

Breakfast at Balmoral on a Sunday morning was a serious affair. Serious because – or mainly because – breakfast was a Scottish invention, like Mrs Hepburn's scones and bannock for tea – and like, you might say, the tartans and wailing bagpipes insisted on by Queen Victoria and still very much in place. Sunday breakfast was the one meal which lay in the domain of Janet MacDuff; and like the doughty housekeeper, could neither be faulted or snubbed by any unwary guest: neither the dieter nor the sufferer from a malt whisky hangover could get away with declining the full fare.

Today, Julia saw as she walked meekly into the long room with its murals of beagles, fox terriers, stags and capercaillie high on the walls and its great fireplace already crackling with a log fire (even in August it could be chilly in Aberdeenshire) that there were few takers for the famous breakfast – and the atmosphere, mirroring the fine veil of dark rain falling horizontally over the valley outside, was distinctly sub-zero. The cluster of wives of minor royals, hanging together for protection, at the end of the table furthest from the royal seat – this a memento of Elizabeth of Austria's throne in her palace at Corfu and adorned with gilded eagles and stags' antlers – appeared to have shown an unpromising attitude towards Mrs MacDuff's efforts this morning. Julia, implored by Harry to brave the morning dining room and bring him up some of MacDuff's specialities (this ploy was also, she suspected, a rather sweet attempt on the boy's part to get her on friendly terms with his cousins and other members of the household, breakfast being the only informal occasion in a day at Balmoral), hesitated before joining them and walked over to the hotplate to help herself to the meal. Janet MacDuff, straight-backed and imperturbable, stood guard here, tongs in hand in the event of a request for a pancake.

'It's intolerable!' Prince Philip's voice rang out like a volley of shots in the long room with its orange carpets and portraits of wounded, disembowelled and dying animals. 'Is there truth in this report?'

Julia felt herself tremble. She faced the hotplate, MacDuff's sternest test of a breakfaster's physique and digestion. Over the sea of scrambled egg, just not too runny and in a chafing dish of heavily engraved silver, a gift to the late Duke of Clarence, homosexual and dandy (and for a time suspected of being Jack The Ripper), from the estate workers at Balmoral on the occasion of his twenty-first birthday, she could see the pepperpot turrets of the central section of the castle, where rooks flew gloomily in the rain. She must concentrate on finding the kipper Harry had demanded, and she raised a massive lid, only to reveal kedgeree, creamy rice and haddock with hard-boiled egg and with a pinch of curry powder sprinkled on top. Julia felt herself about to sneeze. Janet MacDuff would have to be asked about kippers, she realised when further gold and silver platters were seen to contain porridge, and haggis, but no sign of the young Prince's favourite. The very last person she wished to address was Janet MacDuff, after last night's escape on the part of young Jo. 'I'll take Jo a chipolata and bacon and he can make a bacon sarnie,' Julia told herself as she edged towards the cold table, where ham, game and Scotch Eggs lay placidly under the gaze of the waiting housekeeper. 'I'll explain to Harry that he'll just have to do without, today.' And, feeling she had done at least some good for one of the boys, she lifted the giant-size serving spoon and dug into crispy bacon, a side dish of chipolatas – and, espying a dish of waffles, ladled two onto a plate, for Harry and Jo to share. It was while she did this that Julia became aware of the Duke's eyes fixed firmly on her.

'She must go immediately!' were the words which next rang out in the dining room. 'MacDuff, can you see to this please?'

Julia turned as a hush fell over the low-ranking duchesses and courtiers' daughters at the breakfast table. It was she who was referred to – she had no doubt about it. And MacDuff, with an expression of great satisfaction, appeared to think so too, for she darted a glance at

Julia which demanded her instant departure from the castle, breakfast for Prince Harry or no.

The day's newspapers were collected early from Aberdeen Station off the night train from London, and were laid out at Balmoral on a side table each morning at six thirty, ready for the royal breakfast. But in the case of two tabloids, Scottish editions existed; and it was one of these that Prince Philip brandished with righteous rage. Now he did so, Julia had only to look past the cold table at the sideboard where the less palatable diet of the family was daily laid out – and the headlines screamed even in the dull light of this rainy morning. 'WILLIAM'S GIRL-FRIEND WAS WED TO CONMAN' the banners proclaimed. 'DRUG RUNNER FATHER OF WILLIAM'S LOVE'S CHILD.' Huge, blurred pictures of Alison (recognisable), a very small boy and a dark-haired man wearing a gold necklet were splashed across the front pages.

'I'll go and look into it, sir,' Janet MacDuff said.

Julia stood still in the dining room, plates in her hands. One of the sisters-in-law of a royal duchess rose to her feet, taking advantage of the housekeeper's leaving the room, and helped herself to a small bowl of muesli brought north in her luggage from Kensington. The Duke pressed a bell concealed under the carpet at his feet. John, the Head Footman entered – this an unusual occurrence, as the illusion of the Royal Family serving themselves was carefully maintained at breakfast. 'We are two less in the party for church,' the Duke informed John.

'Very good, Your Royal Highness,' John replied. He had his eyes down, Julia saw, as he left the room – but he looked back once at her as she walked to the door as quickly and in as composed a manner as possible, while holding plates of bacon, waffles and a small army of chipolata sausages. If the combination of carrying hot plates and the continuing roar of the Duke's voice hadn't been enough to trip her up, Julia thought as she reached the service stairs that would take her up to the White and Gold Room, then her simple, almost uncontrollable anger, would.

CHAPTER TWENTY-ONE

Julia, Prince Harry's nurse, gave her hand to the Prince of Wales, smiling radiantly at him. The couple, alone on the dance floor, around which stood a crowd of men and women, the men in black coats and white ties, the women in evening dresses, tiaras, necklaces and earrings. Among them were the Queen, Prince Philip, Prince William and Prince Harry. The crowd looked on in approval as the couple, alone and smiling into each other's faces, waltzed on, Julia's blue-grey dress swirling around her. The guests began to applaud, the music changed and David Baron, equerry to the Prince of Wales and rising man in the Prince's household, awoke, heart pounding, in his bed at the Lodge. The image of the dancing couple of his dream was before him, in his ears were the soaring notes of 'Candle in the Wind', the song played at the funeral of Diana, Princess of Wales. But there was no music. In the silence he sat bolt upright, breathing in and out deeply.

The music faded, the images dwindled into shadows and Baron, with an effort, made himself review the events of the previous, long day: his pursuit of Julia's car, containing a young junkie and Prince Harry, to the rehab clinic, Julia's scrambled arrival at the picnic, the images of Princess Diana he'd called up on the computer screen, the banquet, the happy scene in Prince Harry's room, the sense of ease existing between the younger Prince, his brother, the young woman Prince William had brought to Balmoral with her child – and Julia. And now the dream. Baron was not a man who dreamed frequently. Now he knew that even his subconscious was trying to tell him something. He was forced to see what it all added up to. But what it added up to was horrible – impossible.

He went quickly to the shower and blasted first warm, then increasingly cold water all over his body. Shivering, he draped himself in a towel, shaved carefully with a steady hand, dressed, knotting his tie neatly, and went to the dining room for breakfast. Only Sir James Potter was in the room, eating scrambled eggs. 'Morning David,' he said. Baron replied and went to the sideboard to get his breakfast. Breakfasts at the Lodge were less lavish than those at the palace. Baron took a bowl of muesli and a pear and sat down at the table. He did not lift his spoon.

'The Prince is breakfasting with Mrs Parker Bowles,' Sir James told him. 'He would like you to go to him in about twenty minutes' time. Church parade at nine.' He paused. 'You'd better take a look at the Sunday Filth.'

Baron got up, took a copy of the tabloid newspaper from a table by the window and read the story about Alison Walker's drug-dealing ex-husband. 'Oh, Lord,' he said, but his heart wasn't in it. He had on his mind a scandal potentially greater than any the Royal Family had ever been involved in. For either 'Nurse Julia' was a fantasist of the most extreme kind, a woman who so much believed herself to be the dead Princess of Wales that she felt at ease at Balmoral, had copied the Princess's dresses and even wore about her neck a reproduction of the Prince of Wales's signet ring, the gift he had given his young bride-to-be on the eve of their wedding – or 'Nurse Julia' actually was Princess Diana, miraculously still alive, brought back to Balmoral by chance, here under the Queen's roof and now devotedly tending her son. That was impossible, of course, but after what Baron had seen, what else could he think? If Julia were a fantasist, it was Baron's clear duty to inform someone as soon as possible. Such people could be dangerous. And if he had any belief that Julia was the former Princess of Wales, Princess Diana, then there was only one man he should inform – the Prince of Wales, her ex-husband.

He was due to attend on Prince Charles shortly. He flinched at the thought of the ice slowly entering the Prince's eyes, the stiffening of his face as he listened – that complete rejection which occurred when people crossed the lines laid down for them, when things went amiss or unwelcome topics were raised. It was the face of a man with an absolute right not to see what he did not wish to see or hear what he did not wish to hear, and Baron never wanted to see that face turned in his direction. Or hear that cold voice say, 'Thank you, Baron. Will you leave me now?' And how, in God's name, could he begin the conversation? 'I don't like this tie,' the Prince might say. 'Would you select another one for me, David?' To which Baron might reply, 'Perhaps this one might be better, sir. And, by the way, Your Royal Highness might be interested to know that my investigations have led me to think the nurse looking after Prince Harry either believes herself to be, or actually is, your late wife returned from the dead.'

If Baron had hated Julia before – hated her for her growing influence in the Royal Household, for her seeming lack of respect for the indispensable and time-honoured royal protocols, her air of virtue, her relentless, insufferable *kindness* – how much more he hated her now. He had spent time and energy trying to unmask her and, now that he had, he was faced with a horrible, uncanny situation and possibly the loss of his own career.

'I beg your pardon,' he said to Sir James, who had just spoken to him.

'I said,' Sir James repeated, 'that I doubt if we'll be seeing Miss Walker in church today.'

'I think you may be right,' replied Baron. But Julia would be there, he thought furiously. Beside Prince Harry, head bowed, mousily pious. What was he going to do? He asked, 'Does the Prince know what the Filth is saying?'

'I believe so,' Sir James told him. 'I believe I heard – laughter.'

Both men knew Mrs Parker Bowles had the knack of tempering the royal rages, dispelling glooms, lightening cares. She had probably done her magic again. Baron looked into his untouched muesli, at the pear lying on a plate beside it. He doubted if even Mrs Parker Bowles could cope smoothly with the news that it was possible the Prince's ex-wife, believed dead, was in fact alive and living at Balmoral. If true, it would set the proposed royal marriage back by many years.

'Dark thoughts, David?' enquired Sir James.

'Not at all, Sir James. Not at all,' Baron assured the older man. Dark thoughts were not in his job description. Under Sir James's mildly questioning eyes he stood up, went to the sideboard, poured himself a cup of coffee, which he drank quickly, and left the room.

He went to Prince Charles's rooms and entered the dressing room. Mechanically, he took a dark blue suit from a wardrobe, garnered a shirt, underclothes and a tie, and went into the Prince's bedroom. He hung up the suit and placed the other clothes on the bed. The Prince emerged from his bathroom in a towelling robe.

'Morning, David,' he said. 'Any news?' Ordinarily Baron would have some titbit to relate – a maid sent into hysterics by a guest's leaving a prosthetic foot and leg in a shoe left out for cleaning, some 'MacDuf-fery' based on Baron's confidential relationship with the respected, conscientious but somehow comical housekeeper, even an incident involving a corgi. Today, however, he had nothing to contribute but, 'A lovely day for a walk to church, sir. Dry underfoot.'

'Good idea,' said the Prince. 'A chance to walk off the effects of the banquet. A splendid evening, I thought. Did you enjoy it, David?'

'Very much so,' Baron said. The Prince was in a good mood today. If Baron had been less preoccupied and as aware of the smallest nuances of his moods and behaviour as usual, he might have been more pre-pared for what the Prince said next.

'By the way, David, I'll be announcing my engagement to Mrs Parker Bowles in a day or two. I thought I'd let you know.'

Baron was grateful only for the fact that when the Prince spoke he was behind him, helping him on with his jacket. Through dry lips he said, 'Allow me to offer my warmest congratulations, sir.'

'Thank you, David. I don't like this tie. Would you select another for me?'

In the dressing room, Baron picked another tie, thinking desper-ately. 'A day or two' – that meant the announcement could come as early as tomorrow. He must act soon – but what should he do?

CHAPTER TWENTY-TWO

The small church at Crathie had its full complement of worshippers by the time Julia crept in by the side door she had been accustomed to use when assisting her patient in his wheelchair to enter the building. Today, with the aid of two sticks, the young Prince had shown himself to the small crowd of faithful – those whose adoration of the royals enabled them to stand in rain, snow or frost in order to catch a glimpse of the Queen or her handsome grandsons – and had walked to the front pew with the aid of his brother and Captain Lawson, an equerry to the Duke of Edinburgh. Although not officially needed, Julia wished still to keep an eye on her charge; and after slipping into a pew right at the back of the simple little kirk, she sat and prayed (as was the custom in the Church of Scotland: no kneeling, bells or other adjuncts of a 'high' church were admitted here) and she closed her eyes the better to enter into a sense of communion with an unpictured, austere God.

Julia prayed; but she knew her prayers were in vain. The 'two less' in the party referred to earlier by Prince Philip were of course Alison and her son Jo; and Julia was aware, even though she could not see the faces of those directly under the minister's simple pulpit, of the pain radiating outwards from the front pew at their sudden, brutal eviction from the castle. Another chance of happiness gone, Julia thought as the wreckage of the morning came to haunt her, the anger she had known earlier replaced by a deep sadness. And we had all been so happy last night in the White and Gold Room, she said to herself, how can it be that what happens in so many families – an unsuitable previous relationship, an over-boisterous child, a desire to live as the rest of the population does – is punished with expulsion and frozen silence? Why, if this family is so different from others, must we profess an extraordinary interest in its every action: are we really supposed to emulate these puppets in their palaces when the lives they lead bear no relation to ours? But that remoteness, Julia concluded, opening her eyes and craning to catch a sight of the young man she expected to see fully recovered soon (Harry's progress, since they had arrived at Balmoral together, had been remarkable) – that remoteness was probably what drew the loyal worshippers of the Windsors to camp out in the Mall all night in order to observe them in the flesh the next day. They were gods, if tarnished in recent years; and the bread and circuses of Jubilees and the like kept the crowds acquiescent and excited, to order.

Julia, averting her eyes from the straw hat perched at a mystifying angle on the head of Camilla up in the front pew – it looked, the nurse thought, like a collapsed loaf of bread and did little for its wearer – fell to dreaming of another day, another aisle. How often did she recall the sweep of white satin, the long, difficult walk at the side of a stumbling man, the royal faces watching as a girl who had a short time before been the owner of a single dress and none of the accoutrements of wealth and grandeur, became the future Queen of England? She, like so many of her countrywomen – and millions of others the world over – knew the service, the music, the shy responses and the final, glorious return down the aisle of a great cathedral of a Princess. The girl who smiled so radiantly became a part of women's fantasies – but disastrously for her, and disappointingly for her followers, this particular goddess fell from favour with the family which had picked her for the role. The family found her insolent in her readily expressed criticisms. And she –

A hand reached down and touched Julia's shoulder. The service, more like a meeting than a religious occasion, had ended and Julia, lost in dreams and memories of those years, had failed to rise with the rest of the congregation as the Royal Family walked down to the door of the kirk. She saw the Queen, looking expressionlessly ahead; the door opened and a gathering of children with bouquets of flowers went nervously with them to a royal duchess and to Her Majesty herself; their thanks, muttered and almost inaudible, floated out over the graveyard and disappeared in the bright air above the manse. Julia, nodding to the member of the procession who had bestowed a friendly pat, followed him once they were all safely away and into the great black limousines which would carry the party back to Balmoral. The doors of the church closed, the minister hovered, saying his farewells.

Julia and William sat together on a gravestone eroded by time and overgrown with lichen, so the name of the occupant could no longer be made out. The dead were anonymous, Julia thought – but William, who shared the cold slab with her now, never could be. Even Alison, companion of such a brief duration, would become a footnote in all the acres of print about the future King: there was no escaping it, and nowhere to hide. Unless –

'Julia,' William said. He was pale and spoke with difficulty: the cheerful, tousled-headed prankster had gone and an older, sad man sat on in the small graveyard of Crathie Church. 'What should I do?'

'You know it's only for you to decide,' Julia answered quietly. 'But you were truly happy together. Go and find her. Take her away from the pomp and the palaces and ensure the way of life you have been forced to lead is replaced by a better, truer one before you are on the throne. If that's what your heart is saying, do it.'

The minister's wife, coming into the churchyard to collect bouquets left by those children who had found themselves too shy to curtsey and be seen in the royal presence – there were usually several of these and the flowers could be placed on recent graves – saw a plain, ordinary-looking woman and HRH Prince William himself, rising from a gravestone and making their way out into the brae. A waiting Daimler returned them to the castle. But Julia knew her time there was limited, now, and her companion may have known this too, for they sat in silence all the way back.

CHAPTER TWENTY-THREE

It had been a long day at the Braemar Games, and Julia, seated with Prince Harry just below the royal box – Harry, determined to try his hand at tossing the caber despite Dr McLaren's solemn head-shaking on the subject, had pleaded for a gangway seat – found herself yawning straight into the battery of press cameras lined up on the pitch. There would be a joke shot, she could guess that without difficulty, in which Camilla, sitting just above her in another low-brimmed and lopsided hat, would appear to be conjoined to Harry's nurse, one face superseded on the other and sharing Julia's huge yawn. A pithy caption would punningly sum up the boredom suffered by Sassenachs when pressured to come North for the famous Highland event; and Julia would, briefly, become known for her expression of disaffection with the whole Scottish charade. They'd fit in Charles's knobbly knees in his Royal Stuart tartan kilt if they could, she reflected. Only the ancient Duchess of Porchester, up from her stately acres in the Midlands, looked genuinely interested in the athletics, the twirling and jumping and tossing which showed no sign of ever coming to an end. Placed next to the Prince of Wales and with Camilla the other side, she looked exactly what she was, to the loving pair: cicerone and confidante, the discreet receiver of many tales of royal bad behaviour or thwarted marriage plans. If you opened up her head, Julia thought, you'd find a pile of information – on Charles and Diana, and Diana and her boyfriends and Camilla and Charles from both their points of view. There was nothing the Duchess of Porchester didn't know about royal scandals – and the Queen would have been astonished at the secrets the kindly old lady kept to herself.

119

Now, as Harry, leaning on his sticks, went alone at his own insistence down onto the green sward, a vast burst of applause sounded from the crowd and flashlights popped frantically. Harry, shy but determined to show his improvement of mobility, half-walked, half-hobbled into the middle of the pitch and was handed a caber, the trunk of a pine both heavy and awkward to handle. He tried to lift it and the crowd shouted encouragement, their love for the youngest god in the royal pantheon almost tangible. 'You must prevent him from trying to do it,' said a quiet voice behind Julia. The Duchess of Porchester's face, a map of fine lines enveloped by a cloud of white hair, was lowered to Julia's level. 'He'll injure himself – and I can see his parents don't want to make the boy unhappy.'

His parents, thought Julia indignantly. Was the union already assumed to have included the children? But she rose, smiling as politely as she could, and pushed her way through the army of newspapermen and photographers, onto the pitch. The Duchess was right, of course; it would do great harm to the young patient she had nursed with such care, to attempt to toss the caber. And it was gratifying – even if Julia was too modest to dwell long on the matter – that the old Duchess considered there to be only one person who could prevent Harry from trying it. Only 'Sister Julia' in all Balmoral, had the authority to tell the boy what to do.

Harry's cheeks were flushed and his eyes shining too brightly, when Julia reached him on centre pitch. He stood without sticks and held the tree trunk at waist height, grinning at his efforts. The crowd had gone crazy for the feat – if the Prince tossed the caber only a few inches, Julia knew, there would be a frenzy of applause and cheering. But the movement of his upper body, weakened by the accident and not yet back to normal, would damage him, Julia was sure. She walked up to him and said his name – and, like approaching a horse that is pent up, caged before a great race – she spoke gently and did not come too near. This was the time for him to let the caber go – so Julia repeated; and after a minute or so, as the words calmed him, he lowered it to the ground. A spontaneous round of applause came, from the many spectators who had seen the danger; and Harry, Julia's hand in his, strolled off the pitch and out of the enclosure. The day at the Games was over, the yawn displayed by the anonymous carer of the Prince would stretch across the tabloids tomorrow – until, as Julia suspected but did not dare to speculate long, something much bigger than a yawn took its place.

No one would have considered the temperate, calm nurse who walked beside the now smiling and relieved Harry to the waiting Daimler, to be in danger herself, a far greater danger, it must be said, than that of a Prince who threatened his ligaments with premature athletics. Only Julia sensed what lay ahead – but even she could not tell what form or shape her nemesis would take.

CHAPTER TWENTY-FOUR

David Baron arrived later than expected at the castle on the final day of the Highland Games. There were festivities planned for tonight and his employer, HRH Prince of Wales, missed a jacket not worn since the same day a year earlier but essential, in the royal view, for the coming occasion. Baron would need to ask Mrs MacDuff, whose eye missed nothing when it came to guests' discarded clothing (she had been known to spot a thong pushed under a sofa, evidence of illicit amorous pursuits, and pull it forth with fire-irons). Asking the house-keeper where the lost jacket might be found was only one of the topics to be raised this evening; and the importance and possibly inappropriate nature of the other caused Baron to curse his lateness all the more. To make up for his apparently casual attitude towards an appointment with Janet MacDuff, he would have to inform her of the awful truth of his recent dismissal from the Royal Household. The Prince had told his favourite equerry, while being assisted into a kilt preparatory to attending the Games, that he was 'restructuring' his household now his marriage was imminent. Baron would not be needed either at Clarence House or Balmoral – or indeed, at any of the palaces owned by the Windsors. The new Duchess of Cornwall would choose her own staff when the time came; and the servant the Prince had said he could not do without would not be amongst the chosen.

Baron pushed away the scene in which he and Charles had participated, earlier in the day, and set his jaw grimly as he parked the jeep (he had come down from the royal retreat above Loch Adelaide and the vehicle was spattered with mud; so too were his cavalry twill trousers.

Janet would clean them in two minutes flat). He sighed, reflecting he should have brought liqueur chocolates this time, rather than the peppermint creams bought in Ballater, to pacify MacDuff when he told her the news. But they needed each other, he knew – she would go along with his plan and, eventually, become reconciled to his leaving royal service. In the end, the housekeeper might even be relieved to find her name was not linked with that of David Baron. Her reputation, unlike his, could remain untarnished. She could rest assured that she had acted in the best interests of the Royal Family; and she need never know of the other, supplementary motives which had prompted the equerry to make his proposal to her.

The plan was simple. Janet MacDuff had a sister who lived in a cottage remotely situated on the estate, by a bridge crossing the River Dee. Baron would ask the housekeeper if he might borrow the cottage this evening, hinting, if necessary, at a romantic tryst. (She had no idea, he was certain, of his sexual orientation – if indeed she had any knowledge of its existence in general in the human race.) Anxious to assist her friend, she would concur at once; and, all being well, the course of history would change, leaving Baron a rich man. For tonight, by prior arrangement, a fabulous monster would be netted in the home of a humble ghillie on the banks of the Dee.

'I'm positive I sent that jacket to London,' Mrs MacDuff said. 'His Royal Highness remarked last year that it had got too tight under the arms. I thought it would do for a footman at the new residence in the Mall. Don't tell me he's looking for it up here, David: his memory is quite at fault.'

MacDuff and Baron, due to the equerry's lateness, had not settled comfortably as they usually did. They stood looking out at the garden, their silence accompanied by the beat from a minor royal's drum kit on the floor above. Baron had had to splutter out the fact of the Prince's new domestic arrangements along with his request that MacDuff search for the jacket. The effect on the housekeeper had been awkward to witness: she had at first appeared close to tears at hearing of Baron's imminent absence from Court and now she looked belligerent, to say the least. Baron feared he would not be able to keep his secret – the identity of the person with whom he had made the supposed tryst – from Janet. Or, worse, that she had already guessed. In both cases he was right.

'I'm sorry, David, to hear the happy couple have decided to dispense with your services. Can it be that your actions this evening will signify one last instance of your loyalty and devotion to Her Majesty and His Royal Highness? By ridding Balmoral of the intruder who threatens the security of the family, you will have performed an act of valour indeed. For I know, and I know you know I do, of whom we speak.'

Baron nodded gravely while thinking at speed. The day was wearing on, and he must drive to the nearest call box at least seven miles away, in order to avoid mobile phone eavesdroppers. MacDuff, obviously, must not know of the succeeding part of the plan: to her, the capture of the troublesome nurse and her removal from British shores, was the only point of the exercise.

'Yes, Janet,' Baron said. He smiled and half-bowed as if he had all the time in the world to spend chatting in the overcrowded housekeeper's sitting room at the castle. He pulled out the peppermint creams, and asked if Janet's sister would object to playing host to his prisoner for an hour or so before they transported her out of the country.

'I'll arrange it now,' Mrs MacDuff assured him. And, as Baron bowed once more, she added in a worried tone, 'We're all dressing up tonight, David. Is this the best evening to choose, to… to send her back?'

Baron assured the housekeeper that it was. 'After all, she disguised herself in order to deceive us,' he reminded Janet. 'I wouldn't be surprised if she doesn't try it on again.'

'Good luck,' MacDuff called after Baron as he left. She went over to the phone and only when he had gone, did she remember that she had spotted mud on his cavalry twills. It was too late to go after him now – but as she poked her head round the door she saw the last of Baron as he flew down the dimly lit passage. He spoke aloud – talking to himself, she thought, and why not? – he'd had a stressful day. 'Three mill. That's my bottom line,' she thought she heard him mutter as he ran.

Earlier, Baron had stood in a call box, smelling a faint odour of urine, looking out through rain-driven panes to the total darkness of the village street. He began to feed change into the coin box. From the call box window he could just see the sign above the door of the inn:

'James and Jean Muir, Licensees.' The inn was shut; there had been no lights on in the windows of the stone cottages he had passed on his way.

The voice at the other end of the phone had said, 'David? David? What's up?'

And, 'Listen,' he'd said. 'Concentrate. This is very important.'

Baron, after receiving the, to him, life-changing news of his dismissal, had walked briefly in the garden of the Lodge. Then aimlessly he returned to sit alone in the drawing room at the Lodge, leafing through a newspaper in silence. Even now, he ought to mention his suspicions of Julia to the Prince. But the weakness of his position, as about-to-be ex-equerry to his master, made this an unappetising task. From experience he guessed pretty much how the conversation would go. He would state his doubts about Julia and give the reasons for them. The Prince's first instinct would be to freeze him out. He would begin with denial, ask Baron about his health and, not in a friendly way, suggest that he, the Prince, and Sir James had long felt Baron's duties were too heavy for him. Any redundancy payment was likely to be significantly lowered. Whatever decision was made, Baron was fairly certain he'd end up in his small flat in Clapham, a place where he spent very little time, and would, though no longer the Prince's aide, be encouraged to visit the Harley Street doctor normally consulted when those close to the Royal Family seemed to be cracking or showing signs of becoming 'difficult'.

The Family's goodwill would be withdrawn. There were two ways of dealing with those who caused embarrassment: rewarding them for future silence or doing everything possible to isolate them. Baron had a sudden vision of himself in the USA, acting as butler to a Dallas oil billionaire. It seemed that, if Baron did what he ought to, he would be in the unenviable position of the messenger (who got killed) or the man who knew too much (who had to disappear). Justice had nothing to do with it.

He threw down his paper and stood up. He walked out, up the hill and on to the moor, seeking physical action to calm the turmoil of his feelings. He'd worked hard in the position he now occupied. He had started his career working for a firm of up-market London estate agents and, through a client, a famous decorator with a sideline in property speculation, had discovered a member of the Royal Family was looking for an equerry. Baron had expressed interest and been invited to Clarence House for an interview. He first saw Sir James Potter, the Prince's Private Secretary, then the Prince himself. Baron – frank, agreeable, tactful, well informed, a fast learner, appropriately respectful yet never giving any hint of subservience – had been a success. There had been nothing to stop him, in his own view, from eventually becoming Sir James's assistant in the Prince's office and, on Sir James's leaving or retirement, the Prince's Private Secretary. Until the dismissal.

Baron had walked on blindly across the moor, out of sight of the Lodge. His foot went into a hole and he fell, starting up a couple of grouse destined for next week's shoot. He pulled his foot out of the hole and sat, looking up at the blue sky, feeling the wind on his face. He suddenly missed London, and Sebastian. Sebastian, from whom he'd have to keep his secret forever. To a journalist, the story would be too tempting, too potentially valuable to leave alone. He couldn't imagine what it would be worth to the press – millions, probably.

Baron stood up and began to walk back to the house. On the way, a conversation he'd had a few months ago with Sebastian came, unbidden, into his head. They'd come back from a dinner party somewhere and were sitting down in Sebastian's flat, having a nightcap and listening to music. Sebastian was sprawled full length on the sofa. It must have been the thought of the hosts at that evening's party which prompted Sebastian to say, meditatively, 'We'd both better face it, darling. We'll both be working for ever – you acting as some kind of a body servant to a King, me tracking the doings of a load of B grade celebrities, soap stars and minor aristos, in and out of clubs and parties, to Ibiza, Goa, the Priory.'

This annoyed Baron. 'I've got plans,' he said.

'Yes. To get higher up the flunkey chain. Tell, me, what's the difference between them and us?'

'We're not royal. We're not soap stars or models. That's the difference.'

'It's money,' Sebastian said with certainty. 'Behind it all, it's money. And we'll never have any, not proper money.'

'What would you do if you did?' asked Baron.

'It's what *we'd* do, lovely. We'd go away and live somewhere wonderful – Florida, California, Rome, a beach in Thailand. We'd travel, we'd see what the world holds for us. Glorious, glorious.'

Baron returned to the Lodge, ordered a light lunch, selected a video he'd already seen and settled down to a dull afternoon. And, as he pressed Play he realised exactly how much power he had to give Sebastian – and himself – everything they wanted. And knew now there was nothing to stop him doing it.

Sebastian's voice came down the line into the possibly unclean black receiver Baron was holding to his ear.

'What did you say?' A sound like rattling pebbles filled the receiver and Baron cursed, for he hoped the last time, the much-vaunted Highlands of Scotland.

'Three million pounds,' Baron told his friend.

'Christ – that's a lot of money.'

'Can you get it?' Baron said urgently.

'I think so. It'll take a day or two. You are serious? You're not mad?'

'No.'

'Okay,' he said. 'Leave it with me. Don't let the woman out of your sight.'

Back in his car, driving high up over the moors, Baron thought, 'Oh no, Julia. I won't let you out of my sight. I've got you now and I'm not going to let you go.'

His mobile went off. Sebastian said, 'I'll come up to Balmoral.'

'Right,' agreed Baron. He drove through the high and treeless landscape, thinking, 'I'll never let you go.'

CHAPTER TWENTY-FIVE

The Servants' Ball took place every year at Balmoral on the last day of the Braemar Games. Press were rigorously excluded from this opportunity of witnessing the masters dressed up as members of staff, and, although reports came out annually of the fetching appearance of one royal or another garbed in parlour maid or butler's uniform, it was at least twenty years since a reporter in flunkey disguise had penetrated the castle and secretly snapped the party. 'Do promise to come, Julia,' – Harry's words sounded down the corridors of the main part of the great edifice and the unassuming nurse, receiving a cold gaze from Mrs MacDuff as the housekeeper proceeded to the Oak sitting room to join the drinks before dinner customary on these occasions, kept her head down and hurried past. She wouldn't let down her young patient – but the Prince was so much better now and didn't need nannying. And Julia knew she couldn't risk the displeasure of the hosts if she obeyed the friendly order. She would make for her room and stay there quietly until the festivities were finished. For Julia knew she must leave Balmoral, and say farewell for ever to those she loved most in the world – but not, distinctly not, on an evening when travesty was the rule, and rules were, as facetiously as the country's royalty and nobility knew how, flouted and disobeyed.

Mrs MacDuff turned once as Julia sped down the corridor. The housekeeper was in maroon satin and a diamond brooch glittered on her ample chest – for, just as a glimpse into the Oak room revealed the masters dressed as servants, so did the servants put on their best and dress up to the nines for this upside-down evening. The Queen, looking distinctly grumpy, emerged for a moment, holding a mop and attired in a dignified black parlour maid's outfit, complete with frilly white apron and a cap perched on her snowy curls, and Julia flattened herself against the wall, as she had learned to do in the event of meeting the monarch in a narrow passageway. An elderly Royal Highness, got up as the cheeky char of pre-World War Two comedies, dashed out of the warm, well-lit room after her and brandished a gin bottle, supposedly, Julia concluded as she sank into the required obeisance, the curse of the working classes. To her surprise, the Queen gave a loud laugh and held out an empty tooth mug for a refill. Two royal dukes, spotting their sovereign enjoying herself in the corridor, came out to join her – and before Prince Harry could notice his grandmother's near neighbour as his beloved companion of past weeks, Julia muttered an apology and darted to the nearest fork in the long, dark corridor hung with the staring-eyed portraits of dead duchesses and queens. She felt an irrational fear: one of the unconvincing 'servants' – the wife of a Prince done up as a stable lad, hair tied in a red and white spotted scarf – or even the Duke of Edinburgh himself, strangely plausible in an ancient butler's uniform, knees and elbows shining and worn – might come after her. She would be hauled in front of the Chief Constable again and this time she would have no alternative other than answering the new, angry questions. For surely, the official announcement must come tonight, of the royal wedding which had caused such contention in palaces and in the press, amongst priests and in pubs up and down the country. And before it came, there was one person the about-to-be-engaged couple must want to have with them. On this night of role reversal, the eldest son must give a blessing to the nuptials of his father, Prince Charles.

'Sister Julia!' The Queen's voice followed the scurrying nurse down the passage, as she had feared it would. Julia froze: the fork she had approached was no more than ten feet away – but still she disregarded the tradition which insisted that no subject of Her Majesty should show their back to the monarch – or, indeed, leave any gathering before she did. Could it be possible, Julia wondered wildly, that this rule didn't count on the one night of the year when royalty dressed as commoners? Was it socially permissible to show one's back to a Queen dressed up as a maid?

'Have you seen William? It's getting rather late.' The high, unmistakable tones of the defender of the faith, Queen of England, Scotland
and Wales, penetrated Julia's consciousness and rendered her incapable of leaping leftwards into the tributary passage and thence to the
landing leading to her own room on the castle's back stairs. (Here,
doubtless, an army of housemaids including wee Betty and Mary,
applied the full make-up forbidden by MacDuff on three hundred
and sixty-four days of the year: mascara bought in Ballater, pink, red
and purple lip and eye liners brought from a rare shopping trip in
Aberdeen.) There was no way out of it – Julia, aware of her own uni-
dentifiable dress, neither domestic nor royalty – turned as if, she felt,
she had become the enemy indeed, with no place in this castle and no
excuse for her drab appearance.

'Here's Harry – he must know,' the Queen said, and to Julia's
immense relief the small bunch of acolytes and royalty went back in to
the Oak sitting room. She could go now, and at speed. A steep flight of
stairs, once the fork had been taken, rose before her; her limp held her
back as she climbed; and as she arrived on the top stair a hand came
forward to assist her. It belonged to a man who had not changed his
uniform from servitor to grandee; a man so unremarkable in appearance it would have been impossible to recognise him had he done so.
But the air of friendship and kindness of the Head Footman John was
unmistakable, and therefore familiar: no one at Balmoral had taken
so much trouble to reassure the young Prince's nurse, as John. 'I have
something to suggest to you,' the quiet-spoken servant announced. 'If
you will come with me – just in here please.' And Julia found herself
guided into a brightly lit room of mirrors and glass.

It was in a six foot by six storage room in the basement of Balmoral,
its shelves laden with tinned goods and its floors fringed with dozens
of large plastic water containers, that, on the night of the Braemar
Ball, Sebastian Fox and David Baron were hiding. Sebastian, in jeans,
sweater and an anorak, sat on a water container, Baron stood upright,
wearing, as ever, one of his well-cut suits. It had not been too hard
for Baron to smuggle Sebastian, hiding in the back of his car, past the
policeman at the gates to the estate. It had not been hard to distract
Mrs MacDuff long enough with an overturned tea tray to snaffle her

spare keys from her desk, unlock the cupboard later and then replace the keys in Mrs MacDuff's desk. What was hard, and getting harder, was waiting for Julia to appear. Already Baron had made two forays to try and find her. He dared not circulate openly for fear of being pounced upon and required to render some service or other. All he could do was hare round the places where he thought he might find her, then race back to where Sebastian was hiding to report his lack of success.

There was a helicopter waiting in open country by the River Dee, just inside a neighbouring estate where it bordered on Balmoral land. The laird had not actually given permission for this, but his son and heir had, the price paid for Sebastian's suppressing a photograph of the young man coming out of a gaming club when he was supposed to have sworn off gambling for ever. Julia must be informed by Baron that the Prince of Wales wished her to accompany Harry later to the fireworks in the Rose Garden. Sebastian would then whisk her into a car and off to the river cottage. The helicopter would then fly to London, where a hotel suite had been booked. There she would tell her story. Although Baron and Sebastian had worked out the scheme, they both knew, though neither had actually said it, that if Julia proved obstinate they would overpower her, bundle her out into the darkness and drive her to the helicopter anyway. They had come too far to be baulked at the last moment.

CHAPTER TWENTY-SIX

The 'ballroom' created annually for the royal pretence at servitude took place in an outbuilding of the castle, a barn-like structure originally conceived in the 1920s as a rumpus room for those younger members of the dynasty who felt themselves unable to spend every day of the week out on the hill slaughtering birds or deer. There was ping-pong; a mechanical football game with life-size players fashioned out of enamel or tin; large squashy sofas and, daringly installed in the 1930s, a jukebox, never since updated. Paper lanterns and streamers were added, to give a village-hall atmosphere deemed suitable for the domestics, coming as they did (or so it was imagined) from simple rural backgrounds. A pioneer had installed strobe lighting in the 1960s – and by the time the dancing – to Elvis and the Everley Brothers – got under way, the place had the uncanny look of a crazy Christmas celebration, where garlands of cheap coloured paper balls danced wildly in the hallucinatory lighting. Here, the Queen was visible in her maid's outfit one moment – and the next was removed, sucked into blackness caused by a faulty connection unnoticed until the opening of the ball.

Baron, on his first search, had checked to see if Julia was in the annex where the Ball was starting. The local band – drums, saxophone and keyboards – was still warming up and a few couples were dancing. To one side of the improvised stage, the palace piper sat in his kilt, his bagpipes across his lap, waiting for his moment to come. Mostly clustered at one end of the room was the palace staff, maids and footmen, gamekeepers and cooks, in their smartest suits and dresses.

133

At the other end were the palace guests, in borrowed maids' uniforms, footmen's outfits, gardeners' brown coats. There was some connection between the two groups: the Queen, on the dance floor in her cap and apron, was waltzing gravely with her butler of many years; the kindly Duchess of Porchester was laughing up at a handsome young servant in an Armani suit, and Betty the maid was giggling at Prince Harry as she half-helped him to dance.

Baron, in the doorway, scanned the room, peering into darkened corners, screwing up his eyes to see through the swooping strobe lights. He couldn't see Julia anywhere. Sir James, swinging round with Mrs MacDuff stiffly in his arms, called out, 'David! No costume! Go and get changed – don't spoil the fun!'

'Just going,' Baron called back, and slipped away. He went back to the store cupboard to report his lack of success. 'I'll try again in fifteen minutes,' he said. Sebastian nodded. Baron disappeared briefly, to return with a bundle of discarded uniforms. Then he went off to make a second sweep. He briefly checked the improvised ballroom, then went quickly upstairs. Julia was not in her room, or Prince Harry's, not in the library, nowhere. There was only one thing for it now. Go to the Ball.

David Baron and Sebastian Fox, dressed as pastry chef and head *sommelier*, mingled with guests, Fox's face whitened by flour and his tall hat gleaming in the artificial twilight. Prince Harry, blacked up as the castle's chimney sweep, was, apart from a grubby shirt, virtually invisible – and his elder brother, as Baron saw with a sinking heart, appeared to be absent altogether. Mrs MacDuff, resplendent in satin, saw Baron with the trademark napkin folded over his arm and a wine bucket, and pulled him to the side of the dance floor. Fox, gazing at the luminous dial of his watch, cursed the pounding noise of Guy Mitchell singing 'I never felt more like singing the blues' and the exasperating way in which time appeared to be slipping – jumping just like the badly fixed lights. Weren't they meant to have found 'Sister Julia' by now and told her she was wanted by Harry's father in the Rose Garden? Then they were to take her up the river to the ghillie's house. Where was she, for God's sake? For a moment, Fox doubted Baron's integrity – then his sanity. Was this all just a terrific joke? But Baron would find his lucrative relationship had ended, if this were the case – as well as his love life, of course. Three million wasn't such a joke, after all.

'Where the hell is Sister Julia?' Baron whispered in a hoarse shout into Mrs MacDuff's ear. 'Harry was meant to be taken down by her to the fireworks and then – and then – but he's here, if that red hair is his...'

'I don't know, David. But I think she's... can it be, isn't it proof we were right?'

The crowd fell back as a couple took over the dance floor and the jukebox fell silent before starting on a waltz. The woman, tall in a strapless black dress from which her shoulders rose white as alabaster, wore a diamond tiara on her head and cuffs of diamonds on her elegant wrists. Her partner, an under-footman dressed and coiffed as Prince Charles and slightly shorter than the fairy princess revealed in the party lighting, steered his co-dancer with skill – until, as the crowd sighed at her beauty and proficiency, the lady broke away and waltzed on her own. Ecstatic cheers went up.

'Lights!' The voice of the Duke of Edinburgh sounded out above the last chords of the jukebox waltz. Before he could be obeyed, all eyes sought out the Queen, who, if difficult to pick out in the faltering electrical storm, was nevertheless still sharp-eyed herself; and she saw the slender figure, beautifully made up with blonde hair in a style that had been copied – and continued to be copied to this day – by millions of women worldwide. She saw the diamond tiara as it danced, or appeared to gyrate, on the head of the long-gone Princess; and she saw the black, full-skirted gown, the triumph of the royal Canadian tour all those years ago as it clasped the long limbs and tiny waist of the woman she had been unable to mourn. Then all the ordinary lights came on – the figure of the Princess vanished – a groan went up, of mixed relief and disappointment – and the Servants' Ball went on as before.

Sebastian Fox stood in the castle grounds and swore softly to himself. With his tall white hat and spectral floury face he had gone unchallenged by security: too obviously a guest in fancy dress to be suspected of seditious intentions, he was nevertheless nervous at the sound of the first fireworks as they exploded on the far side of the Rose Garden.

A mobile text message had also alerted him to the fact that another newspaper, the last to take up the William Con-gate Scandal, was on its way. Fox decided he would throttle the incompetent equerry when he saw him and, in his haste to call him and demand explanations, he dropped the phone in a recently manured rose-bed. The automatic voice of a twenty-four-hour Bank of Scotland account-holder service, rattled noisily in the earth until retrieved.

Baron and Mrs MacDuff stumbled over moonlit lawns, Baron's wine bucket clanking as he went. Since the lights had come on again at the Servants' Ball, he had to report, there had been no sign of the woman impersonating – so Fox concluded bitterly – the late Princess. The party, now in its last stages, was ending as decorously as it did every year. Only the crowd of Balmoral domestics watching the pyrotechnic display showed polite signs of continued excitement. There was no evidence of any unexpected guest or intruder – such as this supposed Princess Diana must have been. Fox walked wearily towards the main gate. No one would arrest him now: the sense of an ending of an often-repeated occasion lent an air of exhaustion to the night, and even the rival newspaper had flown home.

It was only after the SS *Festen* had sailed for Norway that the absence of Prince William was properly noted, at Balmoral. It had been assumed, as so many of the young royals at the Court had dressed as footmen to attend the Servants' Ball, that he must be one of the many who had sought anonymity by donning harlequin masks – some had gone so far as to powder their hair. Who was to say whether the tall young man who bowed profusely over Mrs MacDuff while presenting her with a glass of champagne, was or was not the next heir in line to the throne, bewigged and disguised on this night dedicated to the Lord of Misrule? William was known as punctilious in the keeping of engagements: surely he would never miss a night honoured by tradition at the castle?

Later, however, some who had been at Clydeside claimed to have seen a young man and a woman with a child in tow as they went up deck and stood with their arms about each other in order to keep warm on this chilly early September night. An older woman appeared to be with them, but she was bundled up in scarves and shawls and no one could remember if they noted her appearance or not. None of the party looked back once, the witnesses abjured, as people did, to wave goodbye to a relative or friend. They fixed their sights on the sky and churning black water, instead, as the ship took them slowly out to sea.

THE END